J. G. Ballard was born in 1930 in Shanghai, China, where his father was a businessman. Following the attack on Pearl Harbor, Ballard and his family were placed in a civilian prison camp. They returned to England in 1946. After two years at Cambridge, where he read medicine, Ballard worked as a copywriter and Covent Garden porter before going to Canada with the RAF. He started writing short stories in the late 1950s, while working on a scientific journal. His first major novel, *The Drowned World*, was published in 1962. His acclaimed novels include *The Crystal World*, *The Atrocity Exhibition*, *Crash* (filmed by David Cronenberg), *High-Rise*, *The Unlimited Dream Company*, *The Kindness of Women* (the sequel to *Empire of the Sun*), *Cocaine Nights*, *Super-Cannes*, *Millennium People* and *Kingdom Come*. His acclaimed memoir, *Miracles of Life*, was published in 2008. J. G. Ballard died in 2009.

By the same author

The Drowned World
The Voices of Time
The Terminal Beach
The Drought
The Crystal World
The Day of Forever
The Venus Hunters
The Disaster Area
The Atrocity Exhibition
Vermilion Sands
Crash
Concrete Island
Low-Flying Aircraft
The Unlimited Dream Company
Hello America
Myths of the Near Future
Empire of the Sun
Running Wild
The Day of Creation
War Fever
The Kindness of Women
Rushing to Paradise
A User's Guide to the Millennium (non-fiction)
Cocaine Nights
Super-Cannes
The Complete Short Stories
Millennium People
Kingdom Come
Miracles of Life

HIGH-RISE

J. G. Ballard

4th ESTATE • *London*

Fourth Estate
An imprint of HarperCollins*Publishers*
1 London Bridge Street
London SE1 9GF
www.4thEstate.co.uk

First published in Great Britain by Jonathan Cape in 1975

This edition first published by Fourth Estate in 2016
4

A catalogue record for this book is available from the British Library.

ISBN 978-0-00-813489-1

Set in Minion by Born Group using Atomik ePublisher from Easypress

Printed and bound in Great Britain by Clays Ltd, St Ives plc

CONTENTS

1

CRITICAL MASS

Later, as he sat on his balcony eating the dog, Dr Robert Laing reflected on the unusual events that had taken place within this huge apartment building during the previous three months. Now that everything had returned to normal, he was surprised that there had been no obvious beginning, no point beyond which their lives had moved into a clearly more sinister dimension. With its forty floors and thousand apartments, its supermarket and swimming-pools, bank and junior school – all in effect abandoned in the sky – the high-rise offered more than enough opportunities for violence and confrontation. Certainly his own studio apartment on the 25th floor was the last place Laing would have chosen as an early skirmish-ground. This over-priced cell, slotted almost at random into the cliff face of the apartment building, he had bought after his divorce specifically for its peace, quiet and anonymity. Curiously enough, despite all Laing's efforts to detach himself from his two thousand neighbours and the régime of trivial disputes and irritations that provided their only corporate life, it was here if anywhere that the first significant event had taken place – on this balcony where he now squatted beside a fire of telephone directories, eating the roast hind-quarter of the Alsatian before setting off to his lecture at the medical school.

While preparing breakfast soon after eleven o'clock one Saturday morning three months earlier, Dr Laing was startled by an explosion on the balcony outside his living-room. A bottle of sparkling wine had fallen from a floor fifty feet above, ricocheted off an awning as it hurtled downwards, and burst across the tiled balcony floor.

The living-room carpet was speckled with foam and broken glass. Laing stood in his bare feet among the sharp fragments, watching the agitated wine seethe across the cracked tiles. High above him, on the 31st floor, a party was in progress. He could hear the sounds of deliberately over-animated chatter, the aggressive blare of a record-player. Presumably the bottle had been knocked over the rail by a boisterous guest. Needless to say, no one at the party was in the least concerned about the ultimate destination of this missile – but as Laing had already discovered, people in high-rises tended not to care about tenants more than two floors below them.

Trying to identify the apartment, Laing stepped across the spreading pool of cold froth. Sitting there, he might easily have found himself with the longest hangover in the world. He leaned out over the rail and peered up at the face of the building, carefully counting the balconies. As usual, though, the dimensions of the forty-storey block made his head reel. Lowering his eyes to the tiled floor, he steadied himself against the door pillar. The immense volume of open space that separated the building from the neighbouring high-rise a quarter of a mile away unsettled his sense of balance. At times he felt that he was living in the gondola of a ferris wheel permanently suspended three hundred feet above the ground.

None the less, Laing was still exhilarated by the high-rise, one of five identical units in the development project and the first to be completed and occupied. Together they were set in a mile-square area of abandoned dockland and warehousing along the north bank of the river. The five high-rises stood on the eastern perimeter of the project, looking out across an ornamental lake – at present an empty concrete basin surrounded by parking-lots and construction equipment. On the opposite shore stood the recently completed concert-hall, with Laing's medical school and the new television studios on either side. The massive scale of the glass and concrete architecture, and its striking situation on a bend of the river, sharply separated the development project from the rundown areas around it, decaying nineteenth-century terraced houses and empty factories already zoned for reclamation.

For all the proximity of the City two miles away to the west along the river, the office buildings of central London belonged to a different world, in time as well as space. Their glass curtain-walling and telecommunication aerials were obscured by the traffic smog, blurring Laing's memories of the past. Six months earlier, when he had sold the lease of his Chelsea house and moved to the security of the high-rise, he had travelled forward fifty years in time, away from crowded streets, traffic hold-ups, rush-hour journeys on the Underground to student supervisions in a shared office in the old teaching hospital.

Here, on the other hand, the dimensions of his life were space, light and the pleasures of a subtle kind of anonymity. The drive to the physiology department of the medical school took him five minutes, and apart from this single excursion Laing's life in the high-rise was as self-contained as the building itself. In effect, the apartment block was a small vertical city, its two thousand inhabitants boxed up into the sky. The tenants corporately owned the building, which they administered themselves through a resident manager and his staff.

For all its size, the high-rise contained an impressive range of services. The entire 10th floor was given over to a wide concourse, as large as an aircraft carrier's flight-deck, which contained a supermarket, bank and hairdressing salon, a swimming-pool and gymnasium, a well-stocked liquor store and a junior school for the few young children in the block. High above Laing, on the 35th floor, was a second, smaller swimming-pool, a sauna and a restaurant. Delighted by this glut of conveniences, Laing made less and less effort to leave the building. He unpacked his record collection and played himself into his new life, sitting on his balcony and gazing across the parking-lots and concrete plazas below him. Although the apartment was no higher than the 25th floor, he felt for the first time that he was looking down at the sky, rather than up at it. Each day the towers of central London seemed slightly more distant, the landscape of an abandoned planet receding slowly from his mind. By contrast with the calm and unencumbered geometry of the concert-hall and television studios below him, the ragged skyline of the city resembled the disturbed encephalograph of an unresolved mental crisis.

The apartment had been expensive, its studio living-room and single bedroom, kitchen and bathroom dovetailed into each other to minimize space and eliminate internal corridors. To his sister Alice Frobisher, who lived with her publisher husband in a larger apartment three floors below, Laing had remarked, 'The architect must have spent his formative years in a space capsule – I'm surprised the walls don't curve ...'

At first Laing found something alienating about the concrete landscape of the project – an architecture designed for war, on the unconscious level if no other. After all the tensions of his divorce, the last thing he wanted to look out on each morning was a row of concrete bunkers.

However, Alice soon convinced him of the intangible appeal of life in a luxury high-rise. Seven years older than Laing, she made a shrewd assessment of her brother's needs in the months after his divorce. She stressed the efficiency of the building's services, the total privacy. 'You could be alone here, in an empty building – think of *that*, Robert.' She added, illogically, 'Besides, it's full of the kind of people you ought to meet.'

Here she was making a point that had not escaped Laing during his inspection visits. The two thousand tenants formed a virtually homogeneous collection of well-to-do professional people – lawyers, doctors, tax consultants, senior academics and advertising executives, along with a smaller group of airline pilots, film-industry technicians and trios of air-hostesses sharing apartments. By the usual financial and educational yardsticks they were probably closer to each other than the members of any conceivable social mix, with the same tastes and attitudes, fads and styles – clearly reflected in the choice of automobiles in the parking-lots that surrounded the high-rise, in the elegant but somehow standardized way in which they furnished their apartments, in the selection of sophisticated foods in the supermarket delicatessen, in the tones of their self-confident voices. In short, they constituted the perfect background into which Laing could merge invisibly. His sister's excited vision of Laing alone in an empty building was closer to the truth than she realized. The high-rise was a huge machine designed to serve, not the collective body of tenants, but the individual resident in isolation. Its staff of air-conditioning conduits, elevators, garbage-disposal chutes and electrical switching systems provided a never-failing supply of care and attention that a century earlier would have needed an army of tireless servants.

Besides all this, once Laing had been appointed senior lecturer in physiology at the new medical school, the purchase of an apartment nearby made sense. It helped him as well to postpone once again any decision to give up teaching and take up general practice. But as he told himself, he was still waiting for his real patients to appear – perhaps he would find them here in the high-rise? Rationalizing his doubts over the cost of the apartment, Laing signed a ninety-nine-year lease and moved into his one-thousandth share of the cliff face.

The sounds of the party continued high over his head, magnified by the currents of air that surged erratically around the building. The last of the wine rilled along the balcony gutter, sparkling its way into the already immaculate drains. Laing placed his bare foot on the cold tiles and with his toes detached the label from its glass fragment. He recognized the wine immediately, a brand of expensive imitation champagne that was sold pre-chilled in the 10th-floor liquor store and was its most popular line.

They had been drinking the same wine at Alice's party the previous evening, in its way as confused an affair as the one taking place that moment over his head. Only too keen to relax after demonstrating all afternoon in the physiology laboratories, and with an eye on an attractive fellow guest, Laing had inexplicably found himself in a minor confrontation with his immediate neighbours on the 25th floor, an ambitious young orthodontic surgeon named Steele and his pushy fashion-consultant wife. Half-way through a drunken conversation Laing had suddenly realized that he had managed to offend them deeply over their shared garbage-disposal chute. The two had cornered Laing behind his sister's bar, where Steele fired a series of pointed questions at him, as though seriously disturbed by a patient's irresponsible attitude towards his own mouth. His slim face topped by a centre parting – always an indication to Laing of some odd character strain – pressed ever closer, and he half-expected Steele to ram a metal clamp or retractor between his teeth. His intense, glamorous wife followed up the attack, in some way challenged by Laing's offhand manner, his detachment from the serious business of living in the high-rise. Laing's fondness for pre-lunch cocktails, his nude sunbathing on the balcony, and his generally raffish air obviously unnerved her. She clearly felt that at the age of thirty Laing should have been working twelve hours a day in a fashionable consultancy, and be in every way as respectably self-aggrandizing as her husband. No doubt she regarded Laing as some kind of internal escapee from the medical profession, with a secret tunnel into a less responsible world.

This low-level bickering surprised Laing, but after his arrival at the apartment building he soon recognized the extraordinary number of thinly veiled antagonisms around him. The high-rise had a second life of its own. The talk at Alice's party moved on two levels – never far below the froth of professional gossip was a hard mantle of personal rivalry. At times he felt that they were all waiting for someone to make a serious mistake.

After breakfast, Laing cleared the glass from the balcony. Two of the decorative tiles had been cracked. Mildly irritated, Laing picked up the bottle neck, still with its wired cork and foil in place, and tossed it over the balcony rail. A few seconds later he heard it shatter among the cars parked below.

Pulling himself together, Laing peered cautiously over the ledge – he might easily have knocked in someone's windscreen. Laughing aloud at this aberrant gesture, he looked up at the 31st floor. What were they celebrating at eleven-thirty in the morning? Laing listened to the noise mount as more guests arrived. Was this a party that had accidentally started too early, or one that had been going on all night and was now getting its second wind? The internal time of the high-rise, like an artificial psychological climate, operated to its own rhythms, generated by a combination of alcohol and insomnia.

On the balcony diagonally above him one of Laing's neighbours, Charlotte Melville, was setting out a tray of drinks on a table. Queasily aware of his strained liver, Laing remembered that at Alice's party the previous evening he had accepted an invitation to cocktails. Thankfully, Charlotte had rescued him from the orthodontic surgeon with the disposal-chute obsessions. Laing had been too drunk to get anywhere with this good-looking widow of thirty-five, apart from learning that she was a copywriter with a small but lively advertising agency. The proximity of her apartment, like her easy style, appealed to Laing, exciting in him a confusing blend of lechery and romantic possibility – as he grew older, he found himself becoming more romantic and more callous at the same time.

Sex was one thing, Laing kept on reminding himself, that the high-rise potentially provided in abundance. Bored wives, dressed up as if for a lavish midnight gala on the observation roof, hung around the swimming-pools and restaurant in the slack hours of the early afternoon, or strolled arm-in-arm along the 10th-floor concourse. Laing watched them saunter past him with a fascinated but cautious eye. For all his feigned cynicism, he knew that he was in a vulnerable zone in this period soon after his divorce – one happy affair, with Charlotte Melville or anyone else, and he would slip straight into another marriage. He had come to the high-rise to get away from all relationships. Even his sister's presence, and the reminders of their high-strung mother, a doctor's widow slowly sliding into alcoholism, at one time seemed too close for comfort.

However, Charlotte had briskly put all these fears to rest. She was still preoccupied by her husband's death from leukaemia, her six-year-old son's welfare and, she admitted to Laing, her insomnia – a common complaint in the high-rise, almost an epidemic. All the residents he had met, on hearing that Laing was a physician, at some point brought up their difficulties in sleeping. At parties people discussed their insomnia in the same way that they referred to the other built-in design flaws of the apartment block. In the early hours of the morning the two thousand tenants subsided below a silent tide of Seconal.

Laing had first met Charlotte in the 35th-floor swimming-pool, where he usually swam, partly to be on his own, and partly to avoid the children who used the 10th-floor pool. When he invited her to a meal in the restaurant she promptly accepted, but as they sat down at the table she said pointedly, 'Look, I only want to talk about myself.'

Laing had liked that.

At noon, when he arrived at Charlotte's apartment, a second guest was already present, a television producer named Richard Wilder. A thick-set, pugnacious man who had once been a professional rugby-league player, Wilder lived with his wife and two sons on the 2nd floor of the building. The noisy parties he held with his friends on the lower levels – airline pilots and hostesses sharing apartments – had already put him at the centre of various disputes. To some extent the irregular hours of the tenants on the lower levels had cut them off from their neighbours above. In an unguarded moment Laing's sister had whispered to him that there was a brothel operating somewhere in the high-rise. The mysterious movements of the air-hostesses as they pursued their busy social lives, particularly on the floors above her own, clearly unsettled Alice, as if they in some way interfered with the natural social order of the building, its system of precedences entirely based on floor-height. Laing had noticed that he and his fellow tenants were far more tolerant of any noise or nuisance from the floors above than they were from those below them. However, he liked Wilder, with his loud voice and rugby-scrum manners. He let a needed dimension of the unfamiliar into the apartment block. His relationship with Charlotte Melville was hard to gauge – his powerful sexual aggression was overlaid by a tremendous restlessness. No wonder his wife, a pale young woman with a postgraduate degree who reviewed children's books for the literary weeklies, seemed permanently exhausted.

As Laing stood on the balcony, accepting a drink from Charlotte, the noise of the party came down from the bright air, as if the sky itself had been wired for sound. Charlotte pointed to a fragment of glass on Laing's balcony that had escaped his brush.

'Are you under attack? I heard something fall.' She called to Wilder, who was lounging back in the centre of her sofa, examining his heavy legs. 'It's those people on the 31st floor.'

'Which people?' Laing asked. He assumed that she was referring to a specific group, a clique of over-aggressive film actors or tax consultants, or perhaps a freak aggregation of dipsomaniacs. But Charlotte shrugged vaguely, as if it was unnecessary to be more specific. Clearly some kind of demarcation had taken place in her mind, like his own facile identification of people by the floors on which they lived.

'By the way, what are we all celebrating?' he asked as they returned to the living-room.

'Don't you know?' Wilder gestured at the walls and ceiling. 'Full house. We've achieved critical mass.'

'Richard means that the last apartment has been occupied,' Charlotte explained. 'Incidentally, the contractors promised us a free party when the thousandth apartment was sold.'

'I'll be interested to see if they hold it,' Wilder remarked. Clearly he enjoyed running down the high-rise. 'The elusive Anthony Royal was supposed to provide the booze. You've met him, I think,' he said to Laing. 'The architect who designed our hanging paradise.'

'We play squash together,' Laing rejoined. Aware of the hint of challenge in Wilder's voice, he added, 'Once a week – I hardly know the man, but I like him.'

Wilder sat forward, cradling his heavy head in his fists. Laing noticed that he was continually touching himself, for ever inspecting the hair on his massive calves, smelling the backs of his scarred hands, as if he had just discovered his own body. 'You're favoured to have met him,' Wilder said. 'I'd like to know why. An isolated character – I ought to resent him, but somehow I feel sorry for the man, hovering over us like some kind of fallen angel.'

'He has a penthouse apartment,' Laing commented. He had no wish to become involved in any tug of war over his brief friendship with Royal. He had met this well-to-do architect, a former member of the consortium which had designed the development project, during the final stages of Royal's recovery from a minor car accident. Laing had helped him to set up the complex callisthenics machine in the penthouse where Royal spent his time, the focus of a great deal of curiosity and attention. As everyone continually repeated, Royal lived 'on top' of the building, as if in some kind of glamorous shack.

'Royal was the first person to move in here,' Wilder informed him. 'There's something about him I haven't put my finger on. Perhaps even a sense of guilt – he hangs around up there as if he's waiting to be found out. I expected him to leave months ago. He has a rich young wife, so why stay on in this glorified tenement?' Before Laing could protest, Wilder pressed on. 'I know Charlotte has reservations about life here – the trouble with these places is that they're not designed for children. The only open space turns out to be someone else's car-park. By the way, doctor, I'm planning to do a television documentary about high-rises, a really hard look at the physical and psychological pressures of living in a huge condominium such as this one.'

'You'll have a lot of material.'

'Too much, as always. I wonder if Royal would take part – you might ask him, doctor. As one of the architects of the block and its first tenant, his views would be interesting. Your own, too ...'

As Wilder talked away rapidly, his words over-running the cigarette smoke coming from his mouth, Laing turned his attention to Charlotte. She was watching Wilder intently, nodding at each of his points. Laing liked her determination to stick up for herself and her small son, her evident sanity and good sense. His own marriage, to a fellow physician and specialist in tropical medicine, had been a brief but total disaster, a reflection of heaven-only-knew what needs. With unerring judgment Laing had involved himself with this highly strung and ambitious young doctor, for whom Laing's refusal to give up teaching – in itself suspicious – and involve himself directly in the political aspects of preventive medicine had provided a limitless opportunity for bickering and confrontation. After only six months together she had suddenly joined an international famine-relief organization and left on a three-year tour. But Laing had made no attempt to follow her. For reasons he could not yet explain, he had been reluctant to give up teaching, and the admittedly doubtful security of being with students who were still almost his own age.

Charlotte, he guessed, would understand this. In his mind Laing projected the possible course of an affair with her. The proximity and distance which the high-rise provided at the same time, that neutral emotional background against which the most intriguing relationships might develop, had begun to interest him for its own sake. For some reason he found himself drawing back even within this still imaginary encounter, sensing that they were all far more involved with each other than they realized. An almost tangible network of rivalries and intrigues bound them together.

As he guessed, even this apparently casual meeting in Charlotte's apartment had been set up to test his attitude to the upper-level residents who were trying to exclude children from the 35th-floor swimming-pool.

'The terms of our leases guarantee us equal access to all facilities,' Charlotte explained. 'We've decided to set up a parents' action group.'

'Doesn't that leave me out?'

'We need a doctor on the committee. The paediatric argument would come much more forcefully from you, Robert.'

'Well, perhaps ...' Laing hesitated to commit himself. Before he knew it, he would be a character in a highly charged television documentary, or taking part in a sit-in outside the office of the building manager. Reluctant at this stage to be snared into an inter-floor wrangle, Laing stood up and excused himself. As he left, Charlotte had equipped herself with a checklist of grievances. Sitting beside Wilder, she began to tick off the complaints to be placed before the building manager, like a conscientious teacher preparing the syllabus for the next term.

When Laing returned to his apartment, the party on the 31st floor had ended. He stood on his balcony in the silence, enjoying the magnificent play of light across the neighbouring block four hundred yards away. The building had just been completed, and by coincidence the first tenants were arriving on the very morning that the last had moved into his own block. A furniture pantechnicon was backing into the entrance to the freight elevator, and the carpets and stereo-speakers, dressing-tables and bedside lamps would soon be carried up the elevator shaft to form the elements of a private world.

Thinking of the rush of pleasure and excitement which the new tenants would feel as they gazed out for the first time from their aerial ledge on the cliff face, Laing contrasted it with the conversation he had just heard between Wilder and Charlotte Melville. However reluctantly, he now had to accept something he had been trying to repress – that the previous six months had been a period of continuous bickering among his neighbours, of trivial disputes over the faulty elevators and air-conditioning, inexplicable electrical failures, noise, competition for parking space and, in short, that host of minor defects which the architects were supposed specifically to have designed out of these over-priced apartments. The underlying tensions among the residents were remarkably strong, damped down partly by the civilized tone of the building, and partly by the obvious need to make this huge apartment block a success.

Laing remembered a minor but unpleasant incident that had taken place the previous afternoon on the 10th-floor shopping concourse. As he waited to cash a cheque at the bank an altercation was going on outside the doors of the swimming-pool. A group of children, still wet from the water, were backing away from the imposing figure of a cost-accountant from the 17th floor. Facing him in this unequal contest was Helen Wilder. Her husband's pugnacity had long since drained any self-confidence from her. Nervously trying to control the children, she listened stoically to the accountant's reprimand, now and then making some weak retort.

Leaving the bank counter, Laing walked towards them, past the crowded check-out points of the supermarket and the lines of women under the driers in the hair-dressing salon. As he stood beside Mrs Wilder, waiting until she recognized him, he gathered that the accountant was complaining that her children, not for the first time, had been urinating in the pool.

Laing briefly interceded, but the accountant slammed away through the swing doors, confident that he had sufficiently intimidated Mrs Wilder to drive her brood of children away for ever.

'Thanks for taking my side – Richard was supposed to be here.' She picked a damp thread of hair out of her eyes. 'It's becoming impossible – we arrange set hours for the children but the adults come anyway.' She took Laing's arm and squinted nervously across the crowded concourse. 'Do you mind walking me back to the elevator? It must sound rather paranoid, but I'm becoming obsessed with the idea that one day we'll be physically attacked …' She shuddered under her damp towel as she propelled the children forward. 'It's almost as if these aren't the people who really live here.'

*

During the afternoon Laing found himself thinking of this last remark of Helen Wilder's. Absurd though it sounded, the statement had a certain truth. Now and then his neighbours, the orthodontic surgeon and his wife, stepped on to their balcony and frowned at Laing, as if disapproving of the relaxed way in which he lay back in his reclining chair. Laing tried to visualize their life together, their hobbies, conversation, sexual acts. It was difficult to imagine any kind of domestic reality, as if the Steeles were a pair of secret agents unconvincingly trying to establish a marital role. By contrast, Wilder was real enough, but hardly belonged to the high-rise.

Laing lay back on his balcony, watching the dusk fall across the façades of the adjacent blocks. Their size appeared to vary according to the play of light over their surfaces. Sometimes, when he returned home in the evening from the medical school, he was convinced that the high-rise had managed to extend itself during the day. Lifted on its concrete legs, the forty-storey block appeared to be even higher, as if a group of off-duty construction workers from the television studios had casually added another floor. The five apartment buildings on the eastern perimeter of the mile-square project together formed a massive palisade that by dusk had already plunged the suburban streets behind them into darkness.

The high-rises seemed almost to challenge the sun itself – Anthony Royal and the architects who had designed the complex could not have foreseen the drama of confrontation each morning between these concrete slabs and the rising sun. It was only fitting that the sun first appeared between the legs of the apartment blocks, raising itself over the horizon as if nervous of waking this line of giants. During the morning, from his office on the top floor of the medical school, Laing would watch their shadows swing across the parking-lots and empty plazas of the project, sluice-gates opening to admit the day. For all his reservations, Laing was the first to concede that these huge buildings had won their attempt to colonize the sky.

Soon after nine o'clock that evening, an electrical failure temporarily blacked out the 9th, 10th and 11th floors. Looking back on this episode, Laing was surprised by the degree of confusion during the fifteen minutes of the blackout. Some two hundred people were present on the 10th-floor concourse, and many were injured in the stampede for the elevators and staircases. A number of absurd but unpleasant altercations broke out in the darkness between those who wanted to descend to their apartments on the lower levels and the residents from the upper floors who insisted on escaping upwards into the cooler heights of the building. During the blackout two of the twenty elevators were put out of action. The air-conditioning had been switched off, and a woman passenger trapped in an elevator between the 10th and 11th floors became hysterical, possibly the victim of a minor sexual assault – the restoration of light in due course revealed its crop of illicit liaisons flourishing in the benevolent conditions of total darkness like a voracious plant species.

Laing was on his way to the gymnasium when the power failed. Uneager to join the mêlée on the concourse, he waited in a deserted classroom of the junior school. Sitting alone at one of the children's miniature desks, surrounded by the dim outlines of their good-humoured drawings pinned to the walls, he listened to their parents scuffling and shouting in the elevator lobby. When the lights returned he walked out among the startled residents, and did his best to calm everyone down. He supervised the transfer of the hysterical woman passenger from the elevator to a lobby sofa. The heavy-boned wife of a jeweller on the 40th floor, she clung powerfully to Laing's arm, only releasing him when her husband appeared.

As the crowd of residents dispersed, their fingers punching the elevator destination buttons, Laing noticed that two children had sheltered during the blackout in another of the classrooms. They were standing now in the entrance to the swimming-pool, backing away defensively from the tall figure of the 17th-floor cost-accountant. This self-appointed guardian of the water held a long-handled pool skimmer like a bizarre weapon.

Angrily, Laing ran forward. But the children were not being driven from the pool. They stepped aside when Laing approached. The accountant stood by the water's edge, awkwardly reaching the skimmer across the calm surface. At the deep end three swimmers, who had been treading water during the entire blackout, were clambering over the side. One of them, he noticed without thinking, was Richard Wilder. Laing took the handle of the skimmer. As the children watched, he helped the accountant extend it across the water.

Floating in the centre of the pool was the drowned body of an Afghan hound.

2

PARTY TIME

During these days after the drowning of the dog, the air of over-excitement within the high-rise gradually settled itself, but to Dr Laing this comparative calm was all the more ominous. The swimming-pool on the 10th floor remained deserted, partly, Laing assumed, because everyone felt that the water was contaminated by the dead Afghan. An almost palpable miasma hung over the slack water, as if the spirit of the drowned beast was gathering to itself all the forces of revenge and retribution present within the building.

On his way to the medical school a few mornings after the incident, Laing looked in at the 10th-floor concourse. After booking a squash court for his weekly game that evening with Anthony Royal, he walked towards the entrance of the swimming-pool. He remembered the panic and stampede during the blackout. By contrast, the shopping mall was now almost empty, a single customer ordering his wines at the liquor store. Laing pushed back the swing doors and strolled around the pool. The changing cubicles were closed, the curtains drawn across the shower stalls. The official attendant, a retired physical-training instructor, was absent from his booth behind the diving-boards. Evidently the profanation of his water had been too much for him.

Laing stood by the tiled verge at the deep end, under the unvarying fluorescent light. Now and then, the slight lateral movement of the building in the surrounding airstream sent a warning ripple across the flat surface of the water, as if in its pelagic deeps an immense creature was stirring in its sleep. He remembered helping the accountant to lift the Afghan from the water, and being surprised by its lightness. With its glamorous plumage drenched by the chlorinated water, the dog had lain like a large stoat on the coloured tiles. While they waited for the owner, a television actress on the 37th floor, to come down and collect the dog Laing examined it carefully. There were no external wounds or marks of restraint. Conceivably it had strayed from its apartment into a passing elevator and emerged on to the shopping concourse during the confusion of the power failure, fallen into the swimming-pool and died there of exhaustion. But the explanation hardly fitted the facts. The blackout had lasted little more than fifteen minutes, and a dog of this size was powerful enough to swim for hours. Besides, it could simply have stood on its hind legs in the shallow end. But if it had been thrown into the pool, and held below the water in the darkness by a strong swimmer …

Surprised by his own suspicions, Laing made a second circuit of the pool. Something convinced him that the dog's drowning had been a provocative act, intended to invite further retaliation in its turn. The presence of the fifty or so dogs in the high-rise had long been a source of irritation. Almost all of them were owned by residents on the top ten floors – just as, conversely, most of the fifty children lived in the lower ten. Together the dogs formed a set of over-pampered pedigree pets whose owners were not noticeably concerned for their fellow tenants' comfort and privacy. The dogs barked around the car-parks when they were walked in the evening, fouling the pathways between the cars. On more than one occasion elevator doors were sprayed with urine. Laing had heard Helen Wilder complain that, rather than use their five high-speed elevators which carried them from a separate entrance lobby directly to the top floors, the dog-owners habitually transferred to the lower-level elevators, encouraging their pets to use them as lavatories.

This rivalry between the dog-owners and the parents of small children had in a sense already polarized the building. Between the upper and lower floors the central mass of apartments – roughly from the 10th floor to the 30th – formed a buffer state. During the brief interregnum after the dog's drowning a kind of knowing calm presided over the middle section of the high-rise, as if the residents had already realized what was taking place within the building.

Laing discovered this when he returned that evening from the medical school. By six o'clock the section of the parking-lot reserved for the 20th to the 25th floors would usually be full, forcing him to leave his car in the visitors' section three hundred yards from the building. Reasonably enough, the architects had zoned the parking-lots so that the higher a resident's apartment (and consequently the longer the journey by elevator), the nearer he parked to the building. The residents from the lower floors had to walk considerable distances to and from their cars each day – a sight not without its satisfaction, Laing had noticed. Somehow the high-rise played into the hands of the most petty impulses.

That evening, however, as he reached the already crowded car-park, Laing was surprised by his fellow tenants' tolerant behaviour. He arrived at the same time as his neighbour Dr Steele. By rights they should have raced each other for the last vacant place, and taken separate elevators to their floor. But tonight each beckoned the other forward in a show of exaggerated gallantry and waited while the other parked. They even walked together to the main entrance.

In the lobby a group of tenants stood outside the manager's office, remonstrating noisily with his secretary. The electrical supply system on the 9th floor was still out of order, and at night the floor was in darkness. Fortunately it was light until late in the summer evening, but the inconvenience to the fifty residents on the floor was considerable. None of the appliances in their apartments would function, and the limits of co-operation with their neighbours on the floors above and below had soon been reached.

Steele watched them unsympathetically. Although he was in his late twenties, his manner was already securely middle-aged. Laing found himself fascinated by his immaculate centre parting, almost an orifice.

'They're always complaining about something,' Steele confided to Laing as they stepped into an elevator. 'If it isn't this, it's that. They seem unwilling to accept that the services in a new building take time to settle down.'

'Still, it must be a nuisance to have no power.'

Steele shook his head. 'They persistently overload the master-fuses with their elaborate stereo-systems and unnecessary appliances. Electronic baby-minders because the mothers are too lazy to get out of their easy chairs, special mashers for their children's food ...'

Laing waited for the journey to end, already regretting his new-found solidarity with his neighbour. For some reason, Steele made him nervous. Not for the first time, he wished he had purchased an apartment above the 30th floor. The high-speed elevators were bliss.

'The children here look well enough to me,' he remarked when they stepped out at the 25th floor.

The surgeon held his elbow in a surprisingly powerful grip. He smiled reassuringly, flashing a mouth like a miniature cathedral of polished ivory.

'Believe me, Laing. I see their teeth.'

The punitive tone in Steele's voice, as if he were describing a traditionally feckless band of migrant workers rather than his well-to-do neighbours, came as a surprise to Laing. He knew casually a few of the 9th floor residents – a sociologist who was a friend of Charlotte Melville's, and an air-traffic controller who played string trios with friends on the 25th floor, an amusing and refined man to whom Laing often talked as he carried his cello into the elevator. But distance lent disenchantment.

The extent of this separation of loyalties was brought home to Laing when he set off to play squash with Anthony Royal. He took an elevator up to the 40th floor and, as usual, arrived ten minutes early so that he could go out on to the roof. The spectacular view always made Laing aware of his ambivalent feelings for this concrete landscape. Part of its appeal lay all too clearly in the fact that this was an environment built, not for man, but for man's absence.

Laing leaned against the parapet, shivering pleasantly in his sports-clothes. He shielded his eyes from the strong air currents that rose off the face of the high-rise. The cluster of auditorium roofs, curving roadway embankments and rectilinear curtain walling formed an intriguing medley of geometries – less a habitable architecture, he reflected, than the unconscious diagram of a mysterious psychic event.

Fifty feet away to Laing's left a cocktail party was in progress. Two buffet tables covered with white cloths had been laid with trays of canapés and glasses, and a waiter was serving drinks behind a portable bar. Some thirty guests in evening dress stood about talking in small groups. For a few minutes Laing ignored them, absent-mindedly tapping his rackets case on the parapet, but something about the hard, over-animated chatter made him turn. Several of the guests were looking in his direction, and Laing was certain that they were talking about him. The party had moved nearer, and the closest guests were no more than ten feet away. All were residents from the top three floors. Even more unusual was the self-conscious formality of their dress. At none of the parties in the high-rise had Laing seen anyone dressed in anything other than casual wear, yet here the men wore dinner-jackets and black ties, the women floor-length evening dresses. They carried themselves in a purposeful way, as if this were less a party than a planning conference.

Almost within arm's reach, the immaculate figure of a well-to-do art dealer was squaring up to Laing, the lapels of his dinner-jacket flexing like an over-worked bellows. On either side of him were the middle-aged wives of a stock-exchange jobber and a society photographer, staring distastefully at Laing's white sports-clothes and sneakers.

Laing picked up his rackets case and towel bag, but his way to the staircase was blocked by the people around him. The entire cocktail party had moved along the roof, and the waiter now stood alone between the bar and the buffet tables.

Laing leaned against the parapet, for the first time conscious of the immense distance to the ground below. He was encircled by a heavily breathing group of his fellow residents, so close that he could smell the medley of expensive scents and after-shaves. He was curious as to what exactly they were going to do, but at the same time was aware that at any moment a meaningless act of violence might occur.

'Dr Laing … Ladies, would you release the doctor?' At what seemed the last moment, a familiar figure with adroit hands and a soft walk called out reassuringly. Laing recognized the jeweller whose hysterical wife he had briefly examined during the power failure. As he greeted Laing the guests casually dispersed, like a group of extras switched to another scene. Without thinking, they strolled back to their drinks and canapés.

'Was it fortunate that I arrived?' The jeweller peered at Laing, as if puzzled by his presence in this private domain. 'You're here to play squash with Anthony Royal? I'm afraid he's decided to decline.' He added, as much to himself as to Laing, 'My wife should have been here. She was treated appallingly, you know – they were like animals …'

Slightly shaken, Laing accompanied him to the stairway. He looked back at the cocktail party, with its well-bred guests, uncertain whether he had imagined the imminent attack on him. After all, what could they have actually done – hardly tossed him over the edge?

As he pondered this, he noticed a familiar pale-haired figure in a white safari-jacket standing with one hand on the callisthenics machine in the penthouse overlooking the northern end of the roof. Resting at his feet was Royal's Alsatian with its arctic coat, without doubt the premier dog in the high-rise. Making no attempt to hide himself, Anthony Royal was watching Laing with a thoughtful gaze. As always, his expression was an uneasy mixture of arrogance and defensiveness, as if he were all too aware of the built-in flaws of this huge building he had helped to design, but was determined to out-stare any criticism, even at the price of theatrical gestures such as the Alsatian and his white-hunter's jacket. Although he was over fifty, his shoulder-length fair hair made him look uncannily youthful, as if the cooler air at these great heights had somehow preserved him from the ordinary processes of ageing. His bony forehead, still marked by the scars of his accident, was tilted to one side, and he seemed to be checking that an experiment he had set up had now been concluded.

Laing raised one hand and signalled to him as the jeweller ushered him briskly below, but Royal made no reply. Why had he not cancelled their squash game by telephone? For a moment Laing was certain that Royal had deliberately let him come up to the roof, knowing that the party was in progress, simply out of interest in the guests' reactions and behaviour.

*

The next morning Laing rose early, eager to get on. He felt fresh and clear-headed, but without realizing why he decided to take the day off. Promptly at nine, after pacing about for two hours, he telephoned his secretary at the medical school and postponed that afternoon's supervision. When she expressed regret at Laing's illness he brushed this aside. 'It's all right, I'm not ill. Something important has come up.'

What? Puzzled by his own behaviour, Laing wandered around the small apartment. Charlotte Melville was also at home. She was dressed for the office in a formal business suit, but made no attempt to leave. She invited Laing over for coffee, but when he arrived an hour later she absent-mindedly handed him a glass of sherry. His visit, Laing soon discovered, was a pretext for him to examine her son. The boy was playing in his room, but according to Charlotte was not feeling well enough to go to the junior school on the 10th floor. Annoyingly, the young sister of an airline pilot's wife on the 1st floor had declined to baby-sit.

'It's a nuisance, she's usually only too keen. I've relied on her for months. She sounded rather vague on the phone, as if she was being evasive ...'

Laing listened sympathetically, wondering whether he should volunteer to look after the child. But there was no hint of this in Charlotte's voice. Playing with the boy, Laing realized that there was nothing wrong with him. Lively as ever, he asked his mother if he could go to his 3rd-floor playgroup that afternoon. Without thinking, she refused. Laing watched her with growing interest. Like himself, Charlotte was waiting for something to happen.

They did not have long to wait. In the early afternoon the first of a fresh series of provocations took place between the rival floors, setting in motion again the dormant machinery of disruption and hostility. The incidents were trivial enough, but Laing knew already that they reflected deep-rooted antagonisms that were breaking through the surface of life within the high-rise at more and more points. Many of the factors involved had long been obvious – complaints about noise and the abuse of the building's facilities, rivalries over the better-sited apartments (those away from elevator lobbies and the service shafts, with their eternal rumbling). There was even a certain petty envy of the more attractive women who were supposed to inhabit the upper floors, a widely held belief that Laing had enjoyed testing. During the electricity blackout the eighteen-year-old wife of a fashion photographer on the 38th floor had been assaulted in the hairdressing salon by an unknown woman. Presumably in retaliation, three air-hostesses from the 2nd floor were aggressively jostled by a party of marauding top-floor matrons led by the strong-shouldered wife of the jeweller.

Watching from Charlotte's balcony, Laing waited as the first of these incidents took place. Standing there with a pretty woman, a drink in one hand, he felt pleasantly light-headed. Below them, on the 9th floor, a children's party was in full swing. The parents made no attempt to restrain their offspring, in effect urging them to make as much noise as possible. Within half an hour, fuelled by a constant flow of alcohol, the parents took over from their children. Charlotte laughed openly as soft drinks were poured on to the cars below, drenching the windscreens and roofs of the expensive limousines and sports saloons in the front ranks.

These lively proceedings were watched by hundreds of residents who had come out on to their balconies. Playing up to their audience, the parents egged on their children. The party was soon out of control. Drunken children tottered about helplessly. High above them, on the 37th floor, a woman barrister began to shout angrily, outraged by the damage to her open-topped sports-car, whose black leather seats were covered with melting ice-cream.

A pleasant carnival atmosphere reigned. At least it made a change, Laing felt, from the formal behaviour of the high-rise. Despite themselves, he and Charlotte joined in the laughter and applause as if they were spectators at an impromptu amateur circus.

A remarkable number of parties were being held that evening. Usually, few parties took place other than at weekends, but on this Wednesday evening everyone was involved in one revel or another. Telephones rang continuously, and Charlotte and Laing were invited to no less than six separate parties.

'I ought to get my hair done.' Charlotte took his arm happily, almost embracing Laing. 'What exactly are we celebrating?'

The question surprised Laing. He held Charlotte's shoulder, as if protecting her. 'God only knows – nothing to do with fun and games.'

One of the invitations had come from Richard Wilder. Instantly, both he and Charlotte declined.

'Why did we refuse?' Charlotte asked, her hand still on the receiver. 'He was expecting us to say no.'

'The Wilders live on the 2nd floor,' Laing explained. 'Things *are* rather rowdy down there ...'

'Robert, that's a rationalization.'

Behind Charlotte, as she spoke, her television set was showing the newsreel of an attempted prison break-out. The sound had been turned down, and the silent images of crouching warders and police, and the tiers of barricaded cells, flickered between her legs. Everyone in the high-rise, Laing reflected, watched television with the sound down. The same images glowed through his neighbours' doorways when he returned to his apartment. For the first time, people were leaving their front doors ajar and moving casually in and out of each other's apartments.

However, these intimacies did not extend beyond each resident's immediate floor. Elsewhere the polarization of the building proceeded apace. Finding that he had run out of liquor, Laing took the elevator down to the 10th-floor concourse.

As he expected, there was a heavy run on alcohol, and long lines of impatient residents stood outside the liquor store. Seeing his sister Alice near the counter, Laing tried to enlist her help. Without hesitating, she turned him down, and promptly launched into a vigorous denunciation of the tomfoolery that afternoon. In some way she clearly associated Laing with the lower-floor tenants responsible, identifying him with Richard Wilder and his rowdies.

As Laing waited to be served, what resembled a punitive expedition from the upper floors caused a fracas in the swimming-pool. A party of residents from the top three floors arrived in a belligerent mood. Among them was the actress whose Afghan hound had drowned in the pool. She and her companions began by fooling about in the water, drinking champagne on a rubber raft against the swimming-pool rules and splashing people leaving the changing cubicles. After a futile attempt to intercede, the elderly attendant gave up and retreated to his booth behind the diving-boards.

The elevators were full of aggressive pushing and heaving. The signal buttons behaved erratically, and the elevator shafts drummed as people pounded impatiently on the doors. On their way to a party on the 27th floor Laing and Charlotte were jostled when their elevator was carried down to the 3rd floor by a trio of drunken pilots. Bottles in hand, they had been trying for half an hour to reach the 10th floor. Seizing Charlotte good-humouredly around the waist, one of the pilots almost dragged her off to the small projection theatre beside the school which had previously been used for showing children's films. The theatre was now screening a private programme of blue movies, including one apparently made on the premises with locally recruited performers.

At the party on the 27th floor, given by Adrian Talbot, an effeminate but likeable psychiatrist at the medical school, Laing began to relax for the first time that day. He noticed immediately that all the guests were drawn from the apartments nearby. Their faces and voices were reassuringly familiar. In a sense, as he remarked to Talbot, they constituted the members of a village.

'Perhaps a clan would be more exact,' Talbot commented. 'The population of this apartment block is nowhere near so homogeneous as it looks at first sight. We'll soon be refusing to speak to anyone outside our own enclave.' He added, 'My car had its windscreen smashed this afternoon by a falling bottle. Could I move it back to where you people are?' As a qualified physician, Talbot was entitled to park in the ranks closest to the building. Laing, perhaps anticipating the dangers of proximity, had never made use of this concession. The psychiatrist's request was instantly granted by his fellow residents, an appeal to solidarity that no member of his clan could deny.

The party was one of the most successful Laing had attended. Unlike the majority of parties in the high-rise, at which well-bred guests stood about exchanging professional small-talk before excusing themselves, this one had real buoyancy, an atmosphere of true excitement. Within half an hour almost all the women were drunk, a yardstick Laing had long used to measure the success of a party.

When he complimented Talbot the psychiatrist was noncommittal. 'There's a quickening pulse in the air, all right, but has it anything to do with good humour or fellow-feeling? Rather the opposite, I'd guess.'

'You're not concerned?'

'For some reason, less than I should be – but that's true of us all.'

These agreeably expressed remarks cautioned Laing. Listening to the animated conversations around him, he was struck by the full extent of the antagonism being expressed, the hostility directed at people who lived in other sections of the high-rise. The malicious humour, the eagerness to believe any piece of gossip and any tall story about the shiftlessness of the lower-floor tenants, or the arrogance of the upper-floor, had all the intensity of racial prejudice.

But as Talbot had pointed out, Laing found himself unworried by all this. He even took a certain crude pleasure in joining in the gossip, and in watching the usually circumspect Charlotte Melville put down several more than two drinks too many. At least it was a means by which they could reach each other.

However, as the party broke up a small but unpleasant episode took place outside the elevator doors in the 27th-floor lobby. Although it was after ten o'clock, the entire building was alive with noise. Residents were barging in and out of each other's apartments, shouting down the staircases like children refusing to go to bed. Confused by the endless button-punching, the elevators had come to a halt, and gangs of impatient passengers packed the lobbies. Although their next destination, a party given by a lexicographer on the 26th floor, was only one storey below them, everyone leaving Talbot's party was determined not to use the stairs. Even Charlotte, face flushed and tottering happily on Laing's arm, joined in the wild surge across the elevator lobby and drummed on the doors with her strong fists.

When at last an elevator arrived, the doors opened to reveal a solitary passenger, a thin-shouldered and neurasthenic young masseuse who lived with her mother on the 5th floor. Laing immediately recognized her as one of the 'vagrants', of whom there were many in the high-rise, bored apartment-bound housewives and stay-at-home adult daughters who spent a large part of their time riding the elevators and wandering the long corridors of the vast building, migrating endlessly in search of change or excitement.

Alarmed by the drunken crowd reeling towards her, the young woman snapped out of her reverie and pressed a button at random. A derisory hoot went up from the swaying guests. Within seconds she was pulled from the elevator and put through a mock-playful grilling. A statistician's over-excited wife shouted at the hapless girl in a shrill voice, pushed a strong arm through the front rank of interrogators and slapped her face.

Pulling himself away from Charlotte, Laing stepped forward. The crowd's mood was unpleasant but difficult to take seriously. His neighbours were like a group of unrehearsed extras playing a lynch scene.

'Come on – I'll see you to the stairs.' Holding the young woman by her thin shoulders, he tried to steer her towards the door, but there was a chorus of sceptical shouts. The women among the guests pushed aside their husbands and began to punch the girl on the arms and chest.

Giving up, Laing stood to one side. He watched as the shocked young woman stumbled into the mouth of this eager gauntlet and was pummelled through a circuit of fists before she was allowed to disappear into the stairwell. His reflex of chivalry and good sense had been no match for this posse of middle-aged avenging angels. Uneasily, he thought: careful, Laing, or some stockbroker's wife will unman you as expertly as she de-stones a pair of avocados.

The night passed noisily, with constant movement through the corridors, the sounds of shouts and breaking glass in the elevator shafts, the blare of music falling across the dark air.

3

DEATH OF A RESIDENT

A cloudless sky, as dull as the air over a cold vat, lay across the concrete walls and embankments of the development project. At dawn, after a confused night, Laing went out on to his balcony and looked down at the silent parking-lots below. Half a mile to the south, the river continued on its usual course from the city, but Laing searched the surrounding landscape, expecting it to have changed in some radical way. Wrapped in his bath-robe, he massaged his bruised shoulders. Although he had failed to realize it at the time, there had been a remarkable amount of physical violence during the parties. He touched the tender skin, prodding the musculature as if searching for another self, the physiologist who had taken a quiet studio in this expensive apartment building six months earlier. Everything had started to get out of hand. Disturbed by the continuous noise, he had slept for little more than an hour. Although the high-rise was silent, the last of the hundred or so separate parties held in the building had ended only five minutes beforehand.

Far below him, the cars in the front ranks of the parking-lot were spattered with broken eggs, wine and melted ice-cream. A dozen windscreens had been knocked out by falling bottles. Even at this early hour, at least twenty of Laing's fellow residents were standing on their balconies, gazing down at the debris gathering at the cliff-foot.

Unsettled, Laing prepared breakfast, absent-mindedly pouring away most of the coffee he had percolated before he tasted it. With an effort he reminded himself that he was due to demonstrate in the physiology department that morning. Already his attention was fixed on the events taking place within the high-rise, as if this huge building existed solely in his mind and would vanish if he stopped thinking about it. Staring at himself in the kitchen mirror, at his wine-stained hands and unshaven face with its surprisingly good colour, he tried to switch himself on. For once, Laing, he told himself, fight your way out of your own head. The disturbing image of the posse of middle-aged women beating up the young masseuse anchored everything around him to a different plane of reality. His own reaction – the prompt side-step out of their way – summed up more than he realized about the progress of events.

At eight o'clock Laing set off for the medical school. The elevator was filled with broken glass and beer cans. Part of the control panel had been damaged in an obvious attempt to prevent the lower floors signalling the car. As he walked across the parking-lot Laing looked back at the high-rise, aware that he was leaving part of his mind behind him. When he reached the medical school he walked through the empty corridors of the building, with an effort re-establishing the identity of the offices and lecture theatres. He let himself into the dissecting rooms of the anatomy department and walked down the lines of glass-topped tables, staring at the partially dissected cadavers. The steady amputation of limbs and thorax, head and abdomen by teams of students, which would reduce each cadaver by term's end to a clutch of bones and a burial tag, exactly matched the erosion of the world around the high-rise.

During the day, as Laing took his supervision and lunched with his colleagues in the refectory, he thought continually about the apartment building, a Pandora's box whose thousand lids were one by one inwardly opening. The dominant tenants of the high-rise, Laing reflected, those who had adapted most successfully to life there, were not the unruly airline pilots and film technicians from the lower floors, nor the bad-tempered and aggressive wives of the well-to-do tax specialists on the upper levels. Although at first sight these people appeared to provoke all the tension and hostility, those really responsible were the quiet and self-contained residents, like the dental surgeon Steele and his wife. A new social type was being created by the apartment building, a cool, unemotional personality impervious to the psychological pressures of high-rise life, with minimal needs for privacy, who thrived like an advanced species of machine in the neutral atmosphere. This was the sort of resident who was content to do nothing but sit in his over-priced apartment, watch television with the sound turned down, and wait for his neighbours to make a mistake.

Perhaps the recent incidents represented a last attempt by Wilder and the airline pilots to rebel against this unfolding logic? Sadly, they had little chance of success, precisely because their opponents were people who were content with their lives in the high-rise, who felt no particular objection to an impersonal steel and concrete landscape, no qualms about the invasion of their privacy by government agencies and data-processing organizations, and if anything welcomed these invisible intrusions, using them for their own purposes. These people were the first to master a new kind of late twentieth-century life. They thrived on the rapid turnover of acquaintances, the lack of involvement with others, and the total self-sufficiency of lives which, needing nothing, were never disappointed.

Alternatively, their real needs might emerge later. The more arid and effectless life became in the high-rise, the greater the possibilities it offered. By its very efficiency, the high-rise took over the task of maintaining the social structure that supported them all. For the first time it removed the need to repress every kind of anti-social behaviour, and left them free to explore any deviant or wayward impulses. It was precisely in these areas that the most important and most interesting aspects of their lives would take place. Secure within the shell of the high-rise like passengers on board an automatically piloted airliner, they were free to behave in any way they wished, explore the darkest corners they could find. In many ways, the high-rise was a model of all that technology had done to make possible the expression of a truly 'free' psychopathology.

During the long afternoon Laing slept in his office, waiting until he could leave the medical school and return home. When he left at last he drove at speed past the half-completed television studios, and then was held up for five minutes by a line of bulk-cement carriers entering the construction site. It was here that Anthony Royal had been injured when his car had been crushed by a reversing grader – it often struck Laing as ironic, and in a way typical of Royal's ambiguous personality, that he should not only have become the project's first road casualty, but have helped to design the site of the accident.

Annoyed by the delay, Laing fretted at the wheel. For some reason he was convinced that important events were taking place in his absence. Sure enough, when he reached the apartment building at six o'clock he learned that a number of fresh incidents had occurred. After changing, he joined Charlotte Melville for drinks. She had left her advertising agency before lunch, worried about her son.

'I didn't like him being on his own here – the babysitters are so unreliable.' She poured whisky into their glasses, gesturing with the decanter in an alarmed way as if about to toss it over the balcony rail. 'Robert, what *is* happening? Everything seems to be in a state of crisis – I'm frightened to step into an elevator by myself.'

'Charlotte, things aren't that bad,' Laing heard himself say. 'There's nothing to worry about.'

Did he really believe that life here was running smoothly? Laing listened to his own voice, and noticed how convincing he sounded. The catalogue of disorder and provocation was a long one, even for a single afternoon. Two successive groups of children from the lower floors had been turned away from the recreation garden on the roof. This walled enclosure fitted with swings, roundabouts and play-sculptures had been specifically intended by Anthony Royal for the amusement of the residents' children. The gates of the garden had now been padlocked, and any children approaching the roof were ordered away. Meanwhile, the wives of several top-floor tenants claimed that they had been abused in the elevators. Other residents, as they left for their offices that morning, had found that their car tyres had been slashed. Vandals had broken into the classrooms of the junior school on the 10th floor and torn down the children's posters. The lobbies of the five lower floors had been mysteriously fouled by dog excrement; the residents had promptly scooped this into an express elevator and delivered it back to the top floor.

When Laing laughed at this Charlotte drummed her fingers on his arm, as if trying to wake him up.

'Robert! You ought to take all this seriously!'

'I do ...'

'You're in a *trance*!'

Laing looked down at her, suddenly aware that this intelligent and likeable woman was failing to get the point. He placed an arm around her, unsurprised by the fierce way in which she embraced him. Ignoring her small son trying to open the kitchen door, she leaned against it and pulled Laing on to herself, kneading his arms as if trying to convince herself that here at last was something whose shape she could influence.

During the hour they waited for her son to fall asleep her hands never left Laing. But even before they sat down together on her bed Laing knew that, almost as an illustration of the paradoxical logic of the high-rise, their relationship would end rather than begin with this first sexual act. In a real sense this would separate them from each other rather than bring them together. By the same paradox, the affection and concern he felt for her as they lay across her small bed seemed callous rather than tender, precisely because these emotions were unconnected with the realities of the world around them. The tokens that they should exchange, which would mark their real care for each other, were made of far more uncertain materials, the erotic and perverse.

When she was asleep in the early evening light, Laing let himself out of the apartment and went in search of his new friends.

Outside, in the corridors and elevator lobbies, scores of people were standing about. In no hurry to return to his apartment, Laing moved from one group to another, listening to the talk going on. These informal meetings were soon to have an almost official status, forums at which the residents could air their problems and prejudices. Most of their grievances, Laing noticed, were now directed at the other tenants rather than at the building. The failure of the elevators was blamed on people from the upper and lower floors, not on the architects or the inefficient services designed into the block.

The garbage-disposal chute Laing shared with the Steeles had jammed again. He tried to telephone the building manager, but the exhausted man had been inundated with complaints and requests for action of every kind. Several members of his staff had resigned and the energies of the remainder were now devoted to keeping the elevators running and trying to restore power to the 9th floor.

Laing mustered what tools he could find and went into the corridor to free the chute himself. Steele immediately came to his aid, bringing with him a complex multi-bladed cutting device. While the two men worked away, trying to loosen a bundle of brocaded curtain that supported a column of trapped kitchen refuse, Steele amiably regaled Laing with a description of those tenants above and below them responsible for overloading the disposal system.

'Some of these people generate the most unusual garbage – certainly the kind of thing we didn't expect to find here,' he confided to Laing. 'Objects that could well be of interest to the vice squad. That beautician on the 33rd floor, and the two so-called radiographers living together on the 22nd. Strange young women, even for these days …'

To some extent, Laing found himself agreeing. However petty the complaints might sound, the fifty-year-old owner of the hairdressing salon *was* endlessly redecorating her apartment on the 33rd floor, and *did* stuff old rugs and even intact pieces of small furniture into the chute.

Steele stood back as the column of garbage sank below in a greasy avalanche. He held Laing's arm, steering him around a beer can lying on the corridor floor. 'Still, no doubt we're all equally guilty – I hear that on the lower floors people are leaving small parcels of garbage outside their apartment doors. Now, you'll come in for a drink? My wife is keen to see you again.'

Despite his memories of their quarrel, Laing had no qualms about accepting. As he expected, in the larger climate of confrontation any unease between them was soon forgotten. Her hair immaculately coiffured, Mrs Steele hovered about him with the delighted smile of a novice madam entertaining her first client. She even complimented Laing on his choice of music, which she could hear through the poorly insulated walls. Laing listened to her spirited description of the continuous breakdown of services within the building, the vandalizing of an elevator and the changing cubicles of the 10th-floor swimming-pool. She referred to the high-rise as if it were some kind of huge animate presence, brooding over them and keeping a magisterial eye on the events taking place. There was something in this feeling – the elevators pumping up and down the long shafts resembled pistons in the chamber of a heart. The residents moving along the corridors were the cells in a network of arteries, the lights in their apartments the neurones of a brain.

Laing looked out across the darkness at the brilliantly lit decks of the nearby high-rise, barely aware of the other guests who had arrived and were sitting in the chairs around him – the television newsreader Paul Crosland, and a film critic named Eleanor Powell, a hard-drinking redhead whom Laing often found riding the elevators up and down in a fuddled attempt to find her way out of the building.

Crosland had become the nominal leader of their clan – a local cluster of some thirty contiguous apartments on the 25th, 26th and 27th floors. Together they were planning a joint shopping expedition to the 10th-floor supermarket the following day, like a band of villagers going on an outing to an unpoliced city.

Beside him on the sofa, Eleanor Powell was watching Crosland in a glazed way while the newsreader, in his florid announcer's style, outlined his proposals for the security of their apartments. Now and then she reached forward with one hand, as if trying to adjust Crosland's image, perhaps alter the colour values of his fleshy cheeks or turn down the volume of his voice.

'Isn't your apartment next to the elevator lobby?' Laing asked her. 'You'll need to barricade yourself in.'

'What on earth for? I leave the door wide open.' When Laing looked puzzled, she said, 'Isn't that part of the fun?'

'You think that we're secretly enjoying all this?'

'Don't you? I'd guess so, doctor. Togetherness is beating up an empty elevator. For the first time since we were three years old what we do makes absolutely no difference. When you think about it, that's really rather interesting …'

When she leaned against him, resting her head on his shoulder, Laing said: 'Something seems to be wrong with the air-conditioning … there should be some fresh air on the balcony.'

Holding his arm, she picked up her bag. 'All right. Lift me up. You're a shy lecher, doctor …'

They had reached the french windows when there was an explosion of breaking glass from a balcony high above them. Fragments of glass flicked away like knives through the night air. A large, ungainly object whirled past, no more than twenty feet from the balcony. Startled, Eleanor blundered into Laing. As they caught their balance there was the sound of a harsh metallic collision from the ground below, almost as if a car had crashed. A short but unbroken silence followed, the first true quiet, Laing realized, that the building had known for days.

Everyone crowded on to the balcony, Crosland and Steele grappling together as if each was trying to prevent the other from jumping over the ledge. Pushed along the railing, Laing saw his own empty balcony fifteen feet away. In an absurd moment of panic he wondered if he himself was the victim. All around, people were leaning on their railings, glasses in hand, staring down through the darkness.

Far below, embedded in the crushed roof of a car in the front rank, was the body of a man in evening dress. Eleanor Powell, her face like pain, swayed from the rail and pushed her way past Crosland. Laing held tightly to the metal bar, shocked and excited at the same time. Almost every balcony on the huge face of the high-rise was now occupied, the residents gazing down as if from their boxes in an enormous outdoor opera house.

No one approached the crushed car, or the body embedded in its roof. Seeing the burst tuxedo and the small patent-leather shoes, Laing thought that he recognized the dead man as the jeweller from the 40th floor. His pebble spectacles lay on the ground by the front wheel of the car, their intact lenses reflecting the brilliant lights of the apartment building.

4

UP!

During the week after the jeweller's death, events moved rapidly in a more disquieting direction. Richard Wilder, twenty-four floors below Dr Laing and for that reason far more exposed to the pressures generated within the building, was among the first to realize the full extent of the changes taking place.

Wilder had been away on location for three days, shooting scenes for a new documentary on prison unrest. A strike by the inmates at a large provincial prison, widely covered by the newspapers and television, had given him a chance to inject some directly topical footage into the documentary. He returned home in the early afternoon. He had telephoned Helen each evening from his hotel and questioned her carefully about conditions in the high-rise, but she made no particular complaints. Nevertheless, her vague tone concerned him.

When he had parked Wilder kicked open the door and lifted his heavy body from behind the steering wheel. From his place on the perimeter of the parking-lot he carefully scanned the face of the huge building. At first glance everything had settled down. The hundreds of cars were parked in orderly lines. The tiers of balconies rose through the clear sunlight, potted plants thriving behind the railings. For a moment Wilder felt a pang of regret – always a believer in direct action, he had enjoyed the skirmishes of the past week, roughing up his aggressive neighbours, particularly those residents from the top floors who had made life difficult for Helen and the two boys.

The one discordant note was provided by the fractured picture window on the 40th floor, through which the unfortunate jeweller had made his exit. At either end of the floor were two penthouse apartments, the north corner occupied by Anthony Royal, the other by the jeweller and his wife. The broken pane had not been replaced, and the asterisk of cracked glass reminded Wilder of some kind of cryptic notation, a transfer on the fuselage of a wartime aircraft marking a kill.

Wilder unloaded his suitcase from the car, and a holdall containing presents for Helen and his sons. On the rear seat was a lightweight cine-camera with which he planned to shoot a few hundred feet of pilot footage for his documentary on the high-rise. The unexplained death of the jeweller had confirmed his long-standing conviction that an important documentary was waiting to be made about life in the high-rise – perhaps taking the jeweller's death as its starting point. It was a lucky coincidence that he lived in the same block as the dead man – the programme would have all the impact of a personal biography. When the police investigation ended the case would move on to the courts, and a huge question mark of notoriety would remain immovably in place over what he liked to term this high-priced tenement, this hanging palace self-seeding its intrigues and destruction.

Carrying the luggage in his strong arms, Wilder set off on the long walk back to the apartment building. His own apartment was directly above the proscenium of the main entrance. He waited for Helen to emerge on to the balcony and wave him in, one of the few compensations for having to leave his car at the edge of the parking-lot. However, all but one of the blinds were still drawn.

Quickening his step, Wilder approached the inner lines of parked cars. Abruptly, the illusion of normalcy began to give way. The cars in the front three ranks were spattered with debris, their once-bright bodywork streaked and stained. The pathways around the building were littered with bottles, cans, and broken glass, heaped about as if they were being continuously shed from the balconies.

In the main entrance Wilder found that two of the elevators were out of order. The lobby was deserted and silent, as if the entire high-rise had been abandoned. The manager's office was closed, and unsorted mail lay on the tiled floor by the glass doors. On the wall facing the line of elevators was scrawled a partly obliterated message – the first of a series of slogans and private signals that would one day cover every exposed surface in the building. Fittingly enough, these graffiti reflected the intelligence and education of the tenants. Despite their wit and imagination, these complex acrostics, palindromes and civilized obscenities aerosolled across the walls soon turned into a colourful but indecipherable mess, not unlike the cheap wallpapers found in launderettes and travel-agencies which the residents of the high-rise most affected to despise.

Wilder waited impatiently by the elevators, his temper mounting. Irritably he punched the call buttons, but none of the cars showed any inclination to respond to him. All of them were permanently suspended between the 20th and 30th floors, between which they made short journeys. Picking up his bags, Wilder headed for the staircase. When he reached the 2nd floor he found the corridor in darkness, and tripped over a plastic sack stuffed with garbage that blocked his front door.

As he let himself into the hall his first impression was that Helen had left the apartment and taken the two boys away with her. The blinds in the living-room were lowered, and the air-conditioning had been switched off. Children's toys and clothes lay about on the floor.

Wilder opened the door of the boys' bedroom. They lay asleep together, breathing unevenly in the stale air. The remains of a meal left from the previous day were on a tray between the beds.

Wilder crossed the living-room to his own bedroom. One blind had been raised, and the daylight crossed the white walls in an undisturbed bar. Uncannily, it reminded Wilder of a cell he had filmed two days earlier in the psychiatric wing of the prison. Helen lay fully dressed on the neatly made bed. He assumed that she was asleep, but as he crossed the room, trying to quieten his heavy tread, her eyes watched him without expression.

'Richard … it's all right.' She spoke calmly. 'I've been awake – since you rang yesterday, in fact. Was it a good trip?'

She started to get up but Wilder held her head on the pillow.

'The boys – what's going on here?'

'Nothing.' She touched his hand, giving him a reassuring smile. 'They wanted to sleep, so I let them. There isn't anything else for them to do. It's too noisy at night. I'm sorry the place is in such a mess.'

'Never mind the place. Why aren't the boys at school?'

'It's closed – they haven't been since you left.'

'Why not?' Irritated by his wife's passivity, Wilder began to knead his heavy hands together. 'Helen, you can't lie here like this all day. What about the roof garden? Or the swimming-pool?'

'I think they only exist in my head. It's too difficult …' She pointed to the cine-camera on the floor between Wilder's feet. 'What's that for?'

'I may shoot some footage – for the high-rise project.'

'Another prison documentary.' Helen smiled at Wilder without any show of humour. 'I can tell you where to start.'

Wilder took her face in his hands. He felt the slim bones, as if making sure that this tenuous armature still existed.

Somehow he would raise her spirits. Seven years earlier, when he had met her while working for one of the commercial television companies, she had been a bright and self-confident producer's assistant, more than a match for Wilder with her quick tongue. The time not spent in bed together they had spent arguing. Now, after the combination of the two boys and a year in the high-rise, she was withdrawing into herself, obsessively wrapped up with the children's most elementary activities. Even her reviewing of children's books was part of the same retreat.

Wilder brought her a glass of the sweet liqueur she liked. Trying to decide what best to do, he rubbed the muscles of his chest. What had at first pleased Wilder, but now disturbed him most of all, was that she no longer noticed his affairs with the bachelor women in the high-rise. Even if she saw her husband talking to one of them Helen would approach, tugging the boys after her, as if no longer concerned with what his wayward sex might be up to. Several of these young women, like the television actress whose Afghan he had drowned in the pool during the blackout, or the continuity girl on the floor above them, had become Helen's friends. The latter, a serious-minded girl who read Byron in the supermarket queues, worked for an independent producer of pornographic films, or so Helen informed him matter-of-factly. 'She has to note the precise sexual position between takes. An interesting job – I wonder what the qualifications are, or the life expectancy?'

Wilder had been shocked by this. Vaguely prudish, he had never been able to question the continuity girl. When they made love in her 3rd-floor apartment he had the uneasy feeling that she was automatically memorizing every embrace and copulatory posture in case he was suddenly called away, and might take off again from exactly the same point with another boy-friend. The limitless professional expertise of the high-rise had its unsettling aspects.

Wilder watched his wife sip the liqueur. He stroked her small thighs in an attempt to revive her. 'Helen, come on – you look as if you're waiting for the end. We'll straighten everything and take the boys up to the swimming-pool.'

Helen shook her head. 'There's too much hostility. It's always been there, but now it stands out. People pick on the children – without realizing it, I sometimes think.' She sat on the edge of the bed while Wilder changed, staring through the window at the line of high-rises receding across the sky. 'In fact, it's not really the other residents. It's the building ...'

'I know. But once the police investigation is over you'll find that everything will quieten down. For one thing, there'll be an overpowering sense of guilt.'

'What are they investigating?'

'The death, of course. Of our high-diving jeweller.' Picking up the cine-camera, Wilder took off the lens shroud. 'Have you spoken to the police?'

'I don't know. I've been avoiding everyone.' Brightening herself by an effort of will, she went over to Wilder. 'Richard

– have you ever thought of selling the apartment? We could actually leave. I'm serious.'

'Helen …' Nonplussed for a moment, Wilder stared down at the small, determined figure of his wife. He took off his trousers, as if exposing his thick chest and heavy loins in some way reasserted his authority over himself. 'That's equivalent to being driven out. Anyway, we'd never get back what we paid for the apartment.'

He waited until Helen lowered her head and turned away to the bed. At her insistence, six months earlier, they had already moved from their first apartment on the ground floor. At the time they had seriously discussed leaving the high-rise altogether, but Wilder had persuaded Helen to stay on, for reasons he had never fully understood. Above all, he would not admit his failure to deal on equal terms with his professional neighbours, to outstare these self-satisfied cost-accountants and marketing managers.

As his sons wandered sleepily into the room Helen remarked, 'Perhaps we could move to a higher floor.'

Shaving his chin, Wilder pondered this last comment of his wife's. The frail plea had a particular significance, as if some long-standing ambition had been tapped inside his head. Helen, of course, was thinking in terms of social advancement, of moving in effect to a 'better neighbourhood', away from this lower-class suburb to those smarter residential districts somewhere between the 15th and 30th floors, where the corridors were clean and the children would not have to play in the streets, where tolerance and sophistication civilized the air.

Wilder had something different in mind. As he listened to Helen's quiet voice, murmuring to her two sons as if speaking to them from inside a deep dream, he examined himself in the mirror. Like a prize-fighter reassuring himself before a match, he patted the muscles of his stomach and shoulders. In the mental as well as the physical sense, he was almost certainly the strongest man in the building, and Helen's lack of spirit annoyed him. He realized that he had no real means of coping with this kind of passivity. His response to it was still framed by his upbringing, by an over-emotional mother who had loved him devotedly through the longest possible childhood she could arrange and thereby given Wilder what he always thought of as his unshakeable self-confidence. She had separated from Wilder's father – a shadowy figure of disreputable background – when he was a small child. The second marriage, to a pleasant but passive accountant and chess enthusiast, had been wholly dominated by the relationship between the mother and her bullock-like son. When he met his future wife Wilder naively believed that he wanted to pass on these advantages to Helen, to look after her and provide an endless flow of security and good humour. Of course, as he realized now, no one ever changed, and for all his abundant self-confidence he needed to be looked after just as much as ever. Once or twice, in unguarded moments during the early days of their marriage, he had attempted to play the childish games he had enjoyed with his mother. But Helen had not been able to bring herself to treat Wilder like her son. For her part, Wilder guessed, love and care were the last things she really wanted. Perhaps the breakdown of life in the high-rise would fulfil her unconscious expectations more than she realized.

As he massaged his cheeks Wilder listened to the air humming erratically in the air-conditioning flues behind the shower stall, pumped all the way down from the roof of the building thirty-nine floors above. He watched the water emerge from the tap. This too had made its long descent from the reservoirs on the roof, running down the immense internal wells riven through the apartment block, like icy streams percolating through a subterranean cavern.

His determination to make the documentary had a strong personal bias, part of a calculated attempt to come to terms with the building, meet the physical challenge it presented to him, and then dominate it. For some time now he had known that he was developing a powerful phobia about the high-rise. He was constantly aware of the immense weight of concrete stacked above him, and the sense that his body was the focus of the lines of force running through the building, almost as if Anthony Royal had deliberately designed his body to be held within their grip. At night, as he lay beside his sleeping wife, he would often wake from an uneasy dream into the suffocating bedroom, conscious of each of the 999 other apartments pressing on him through the walls and ceiling, forcing the air from his chest. He was sure that he had drowned the Afghan, not because he disliked the dog particularly or wanted to upset its owner, but to revenge himself on the upper storeys of the building. He had seized the dog in the darkness when it blundered into the pool. Giving in to a cruel but powerful impulse, he had pulled it below the water. As he held its galvanized and thrashing body under the surface, in a strange way he had been struggling with the building itself. Thinking of those distant heights, Wilder took his shower, turning the cold tap on full and letting the icy jet roar across his chest and loins. Where Helen had begun to falter, he felt more determined, like a climber who has at long last reached the foot of the mountain he has prepared all his life to scale.

5

THE VERTICAL CITY

Whatever plans he might devise for his ascent, whatever route to the summit, it was soon obvious to Wilder that at its present rate of erosion little of the high-rise would be left. Almost everything possible was going wrong with the services. He helped Helen straighten the apartment, and tried to jerk some sense of vitality into his dormant family by drawing blinds and moving noisily around the rooms.

Wilder found it difficult to revive them. At five-minute intervals the air-conditioning ceased to work, and in the warm summer weather the apartment was heavy with stagnant air. Wilder noticed that he had already begun to accept the foetid atmosphere as normal. Helen told him that she had heard a rumour from the other residents that dog excrement had been deliberately dropped into the air-conditioning flues by the upper-level tenants. Strong winds circulated around the open plazas of the development project, buffeting the lower floors of the apartment building as they swirled through the concrete legs. Wilder opened the windows, hoping for some fresh air, but the apartment soon filled with dust and powdered cement. The ashy film already covered the tops of cupboards and bookshelves.

By the late afternoon the residents began to return from their offices. The elevators were noisy and overcrowded. Three of them were now out of order, and the remainder were jammed with impatient tenants trying to reach their floors. From the open door of his apartment Wilder watched his neighbours jostle each other aggressively like bad-tempered miners emerging from their pit-cages. They strode past him, briefcases and handbags wielded like the instruments of an over-nervous body armour.

On an impulse Wilder decided to test his rights of free passage around the building, and his access to all its services, particularly the swimming-pool on the 35th floor and the children's sculpture-garden on the observation roof. Taking his camera, he set out for the roof with the older of his two sons. However, he soon found that the high-speed elevators were either out of order, under repair, or kept permanently at the top floors with their doors jammed open. The only access to them was through the private outside entrance to which Wilder did not have a key.

All the more determined now to reach the roof, Wilder waited for one of the intermediate elevators which would carry them as far as the 35th floor. When it arrived he pushed his way into the crowded cabin, surrounded by passengers who stared down at Wilder's six-year-old son with unfeigned hostility. At the 23rd floor the elevator refused to move any further. The passengers scrummaged their way out, drumming their briefcases against the closed doors of the elevators in what seemed to be a ritual display of temper.

Wilder set off up the stairs, carrying his small son in his arms. With his powerful physique, he was strong enough to climb all the way to the roof. Two floors above, however, the staircase was blocked by a group of local residents – among them the offensive young orthodontic surgeon who was Robert Laing's neighbour – trying to free a garbage-disposal chute. Suspicious that they might be tampering with the air-conditioning ducts, Wilder pushed through them, but was briskly shouldered aside by a man he recognized as a newsreader for a rival television company.

'This staircase is closed, Wilder! Can't you get the point?'

'What?' Wilder was amazed by this effrontery. 'How do you mean?'

'*Closed!* What are you doing up here, anyway?'

The two men squared up to each other. Amused by the announcer's aggressive manner, Wilder lifted the camera as if to film his florid face. When Crosland waved him away imperiously, Wilder was tempted to knock the man down. Not wishing to upset his son, who was nervous enough already in this harsh atmosphere, he retreated to the elevator and returned to the lower floors.

The confrontation, however minor, had unsettled Wilder. Ignoring Helen, he prowled around the apartment, swinging the camera to and fro. He felt excited in a confused way, partly by his plans for the documentary, but also by the growing atmosphere of collision and hostility.

From the balcony he watched the huge, Alcatraz blocks of the nearby high-rises. The material about these buildings, visual and sociological, was almost limitless. They would film the exteriors from a helicopter, and from the nearest block four hundred yards away – in his mind's eye he could already see a long, sixty-second zoom, slowly moving from the whole building in frame to a close-up of a single apartment, one cell in this nightmare termitary.

The first half of the programme would examine life in the high-rise in terms of its design errors and minor irritations, while the remainder would then look at the psychology of living in a community of two thousand people boxed up into the sky – everything from the incidence of crime, divorce and sexual misdemeanours to the turnover of residents, their health, the frequency of insomnia and other psychosomatic disorders. All the evidence accumulated over several decades cast a critical light on the high-rise as a viable social structure, but cost-effectiveness in the area of public housing and high profitability in the private sector kept pushing these vertical townships into the sky against the real needs of their occupants.

The psychology of high-rise life had been exposed with damning results. The absence of humour, for example, had always struck Wilder as the single most significant feature – all research by investigators confirmed that the tenants of high-rises made no jokes about them. In a strict sense, life there was 'eventless'. On the basis of his own experience, Wilder was convinced that the high-rise apartment was an insufficiently flexible shell to provide the kind of home which encouraged activities, as distinct from somewhere to eat and sleep. Living in high-rises required a special type of behaviour, one that was acquiescent, restrained, even perhaps slightly mad. A psychotic would have a ball here, Wilder reflected. Vandalism had plagued these slab and tower blocks since their inception. Every torn-out piece of telephone equipment, every handle wrenched off a fire safety door, every kicked-in electricity meter represented a stand against decerebration.

What angered Wilder most of all about life in the apartment building was the way in which an apparently homogeneous collection of high-income professional people had split into three distinct and hostile camps. The old social subdivisions, based on power, capital and self-interest, had reasserted themselves here as anywhere else.

In effect, the high-rise had already divided itself into the three classical social groups, its lower, middle and upper classes. The 10th-floor shopping mall formed a clear boundary between the lower nine floors, with their 'proletariat' of film technicians, air-hostesses and the like, and the middle section of the high-rise, which extended from the 10th floor to the swimming-pool and restaurant deck on the 35th. This central two-thirds of the apartment building formed its middle class, made up of self-centred but basically docile members of the professions – the doctors and lawyers, accountants and tax specialists who worked, not for themselves, but for medical institutes and large corporations. Puritan and self-disciplined, they had all the cohesion of those eager to settle for second best.

Above them, on the top five floors of the high-rise, was its upper class, the discreet oligarchy of minor tycoons and entrepreneurs, television actresses and careerist academics, with their high-speed elevators and superior services, their carpeted staircases. It was they who set the pace of the building. It was their complaints which were acted upon first, and it was they who subtly dominated life within the high-rise, deciding when the children could use the swimming-pools and roof garden, the menus in the restaurant and the high charges that kept out almost everyone but themselves. Above all, it was their subtle patronage that kept the middle ranks in line, this constantly dangling carrot of friendship and approval.

The thought of these exclusive residents, as high above him in their top-floor redoubts as any feudal lord above a serf, filled Wilder with a growing sense of impatience and resentment. However, it was difficult to organize any kind of counter-attack. It would be easy enough to play the populist leader and become the spokesman of his neighbours on the lower floors, but they lacked any cohesion or self-interest; they would be no match for the well-disciplined professional people in the central section of the apartment building. There was a latent easy-goingness about them, an inclination to tolerate an undue amount of interference before simply packing up and moving on. In short, their territorial instinct, in its psychological and social senses, had atrophied to the point where they were ripe for exploitation.

To rally his neighbours Wilder needed something that would give them a strong feeling of identity. The television documentary would do this perfectly and in terms, moreover, which they could understand. The documentary would dramatize all their resentments, and expose the way in which the services and facilities were being abused by the upper-level tenants. It might even be necessary to foment trouble surreptitiously, to exaggerate the tensions present in the high-rise.

However, as Wilder soon discovered, the shape of his documentary was already being determined.

Fired by his resolve to fight back, Wilder decided to give his wife and children a break from his ceaseless pacing. The air-conditioning now worked for only five minutes in each hour, and by dusk the apartment was stuffy and humid. The noise of over-loud conversations and record-players at full volume reverberated off the balconies above them. Helen Wilder moved along the already closed windows, her small hands pressed numbly against the latches as if trying to push away the night.

Too preoccupied to help her, Wilder set off with a towel and swimming trunks to the pool on the 10th floor. A few telephone calls to his neighbours on the lower floors had confirmed that they were keen to take part in the documentary, but Wilder needed participants from the upper and middle levels of the high-rise.

The out-of-order elevators had still not been repaired, and Wilder took to the stairs. Sections of the staircase had already been turned into a garbage-well by the residents above. Broken glass littered the steps, cutting his shoes.

The shopping mall was crowded with people, milling about and talking at the tops of their voices as if waiting for a political rally to start. Usually deserted at this hour, the swimming-pool was packed with residents playing the fool in the water, pushing each other off the tiled verge and splashing the changing stalls. The attendant had gone, abandoning his booth, and already the pool was beginning to look neglected, discarded towels lying in the gutters.

In the showers Wilder recognized Robert Laing. Although the doctor turned his back on him Wilder ignored the rebuff and stood under the next spray. The two men spoke briefly but in non-committal terms. Wilder had always found Laing good company, with his keen eye for any passing young woman, but today he was being standoffish. Like everyone else he had been affected by the atmosphere of confrontation.

'Have the police arrived yet?' Wilder asked above the noise as they walked to the diving-boards.

'No – are you expecting them?' Laing seemed genuinely surprised.

'They'll want to question the witnesses. What happened, in fact? Was he pushed? His wife looks hefty enough – perhaps she wanted a quick divorce?'

Laing smiled patiently, as if this remark in doubtful taste was all he expected of Wilder. His sharp eyes were deliberately vague, and remained closed to any probing. 'I know nothing about the accident, Wilder. It may have been suicide, I suppose. Are you personally concerned?'

'Aren't you, Laing? It's odd that a man can fall from a window forty floors above the ground without there being any kind of investigation …'

Laing stepped on to the diving board. His body was unusually well muscled, Wilder noticed, almost as if he had been taking a good deal of recent exercise, doing dozens of push-ups.

Laing waited for a clear space in the crowded water. 'I think we can rely on his neighbours to look after everything.'

Wilder lifted his voice. 'I've begun planning the television documentary – his death would make a good starting point.'

Laing looked down at Wilder with sudden interest. He shook his head firmly. 'I'd forget all about it – if I were you, Wilder.' He stepped to the end of the board, sprang twice and made a hard, neat dive into the yellowing water.

Swimming by himself at the shallow end of the pool. Wilder watched Laing and his party of friends playing about in the deep end. Previously Wilder would have joined them, particularly as there were two attractive women in the group – Charlotte Melville, whom he had not seen for several days about their projected parents' association, and the tyro alcoholic Eleanor Powell. Wilder had obviously been excluded. Laing's pointed use of his surname marked the distance between them, like his vagueness about the dead jeweller, and his sidestepping of the television documentary, in which he had once been keenly interested – if anything, Laing's approval had inspired Wilder to develop the idea into a provisional treatment. Presumably Laing, with his excessive need for privacy, had no wish to see the collective folly of the residents, their childish squabbles and jealousies, exposed on the nation's television screens.

Or was there some other impulse at work – a need to shut away, most of all from oneself, any realization of what was actually happening in the high-rise, so that events there could follow their own logic and get even more out of hand? For all his own professed enthusiasm about the documentary, Wilder knew that he had never discussed it with anyone who did not live inside the apartment building. Even Helen, talking to her mother that afternoon on the telephone, had said vaguely, 'Everything's fine. There's some slight trouble with the air-conditioning, but it's being fixed.'

This growing defiance of reality no longer surprised Wilder. The decision that the chaos within the high-rise was a matter for the residents themselves explained the mystery of the dead jeweller. At least a thousand people must have seen the body – Wilder remembered stepping on to the balcony and being startled, not by the sight of the dead man, but by the huge audience reaching up to the sky. Had anyone notified the police? He had taken it for granted, but now he was less sure. Wilder found it hard to believe that this sophisticated and self-important man would commit suicide. Yet no one was in the least concerned, accepting the possibility of murder in the same way that the swimmers in the pool accepted the wine bottles and beer cans rolling around the tiled floor under their feet.

During the evening, Wilder's speculations took second place to the struggle to preserve his sanity. After settling the two boys in their bedroom, he and his wife sat down to dinner, only to find that a sudden electricity failure had plunged them into darkness. Sitting opposite each other at the dining-room table, they listened to the continuous noise from the corridor, their neighbours arguing in the elevator lobby, transistors blaring through open apartment doors.

Helen began to laugh, relaxing for the first time in weeks. 'Dick, it's a huge children's party that's got out of hand.' She reached out to calm Wilder. In the faint light that crossed the room from the nearby high-rise her slim face had an almost unreal calm, as if she no longer felt herself to be part of the events taking place around her.

Restraining his temper, Wilder hunched heavily in the darkness over the table. He was tempted more than once to plunge his fist into the soup. When the lights returned he tried to telephone the building manager, but the switchboard was jammed with calls. At last a recorded voice told him that the manager had fallen ill, and that all complaints would be played through and noted for future attention.

'My God, he's actually going to listen to all these tapes – there must be miles of them ...'

'Are you sure?' Helen was giggling to herself. 'Perhaps no one else minds. You're the only one.'

The tampering with the electricity system had affected the air-conditioning. Dust was spurting from the vents in the walls. Exasperated, Wilder drove his fists together. Like a huge and aggressive malefactor, the high-rise was determined to inflict every conceivable hostility upon them. Wilder tried to close the grilles, but within minutes they were forced to take refuge on the balcony. Their neighbours were crowded against their railings, craning up at the roof as if hoping to catch sight of those responsible.

Leaving his wife, who was wandering light-heartedly around the apartment and smiling at the spurting dust, Wilder went out into the corridor. All the elevators were stationary in the upper section of the building. A large group of his neighbours had gathered in the elevator lobby, pounding rhythmically on the doors and complaining about various provocative acts by the residents on the floors above.

Wilder pushed his way towards the centre, where two airline pilots were standing on a lobby sofa and selecting the members of a raiding party. Wilder waited his turn, trying to catch their attention, until he realized from the excited talk around him that their mission consisted solely of going up to the 35th floor and publicly urinating into the water.

Wilder was about to argue with them, warning that a childish act of this kind would be counter-productive. Until they were organized the notion of a punitive expedition was absurd, as they were far too exposed to retaliation. However, at the last moment he turned away. He stood by the doors to the staircase, aware that he no longer felt committed to this crowd of impulsive tenants egging each other on to a futile exercise. Their real opponent was not the hierarchy of residents in the heights far above them, but the image of the building in their own minds, the multiplying layers of concrete that anchored them to the floor.

A cheer went up, followed by a chorus of catcalls. An elevator was descending from the 35th floor, the indicator numerals flashing from right to left. While it approached, Wilder thought of Helen and the two boys – he knew already that his decision to dissociate himself from his neighbours had nothing to do with any feelings of concern for his wife and children.

The elevator reached the 2nd floor and stopped. As the doors opened there was a sudden hush. Lying on the floor of the cabin was the barely conscious figure of one of Wilder's neighbours, a homosexual air-traffic controller who dined regularly in the 35th-floor restaurant. He turned his bruised face away from the watching crowd and tried to button the shirt torn from his chest. Seeing him clearly as the crowd stepped back, awed by this evidence of open violence, Wilder heard someone say that two more floors, the 5th and 8th, were now in darkness.

6

DANGER IN THE STREETS OF THE SKY

All day Richard Wilder had been preparing for his ascent. After the noise-filled night, which he had spent calming his sons and his giggling wife, Wilder left for the television studios. Once there, he cancelled his appointments and told his secretary that he would be away for the next few days. While he spoke, Wilder was barely aware of this puzzled young woman or his curious colleagues in the nearby offices – he had shaved only the left side of his face, and had not changed his clothes since the previous day. Tired out, he briefly fell asleep at his desk, watched by his secretary as he slumped snoring across his unread correspondence. After no more than an hour at the studios, he packed his briefcase and returned to the high-rise.

For Wilder, this brief period away from the apartment building was almost dreamlike in its unreality. He left his car in the parking-lot without locking it and walked towards the entrance, a growing sense of relief coming over him. Even the debris scattered at the foot of the building, the empty bottles and garbage-stained cars with their broken windscreens, in a strange way merely reinforced his conviction that the only real events in his life were those taking place within the high-rise.

Although it was after eleven o'clock, Helen and the children were still asleep. A film of white dust covered the furniture in the lounge and bedrooms, as if he had returned to the apartment and its three sleepers after an immense period of time had condensed around them like a stone frost. Wilder had blocked the air-conditioning vents during the night, and the apartment was without sound or movement. Wilder looked down at his wife, lying on the bed surrounded by the children's books she was reviewing. Aware that he would be leaving her in a few hours, he regretted that she was too weak to come with him. They might have climbed the high-rise together.

Trying to think more clearly about his ascent, Wilder began to clean the apartment. He stepped out on to the balcony and swept up the cigarette butts and broken glass, condoms and torn newspapers thrown down from the floors above. He could no longer remember when he had made his decision to climb the building, and had little idea of what exactly he would do when he finally got there. He was also well aware of the disparity between the simple business of climbing to the roof – a matter of pressing an elevator button – and the mythologized version of this ascent that had taken over his mind.

This same surrender to a logic more powerful than reason was evident in the behaviour of Wilder's neighbours. In the elevator lobby he listened to the latest rumours. Earlier that morning there had been a serious brawl between the 9th and 11th-floor tenants. The 10th-floor concourse was now a no-man's-land between two warring factions, the residents of the lower nine floors and those in the middle section of the building. Despite the harassment and increasing violence, no one was surprised by these events. The routines of daily life within the high-rise, the visits to the supermarket, liquor store and hairdressing salon continued as before. In some way the high-rise was able to accommodate this double logic. Even the tone of voice of his neighbours as they described these outbreaks of hostility was calm and matter-of-fact, like that of civilians in a war-torn city dealing with yet another air-raid. For the first time it occurred to Wilder that the residents enjoyed this breakdown of its services, and the growing confrontation between themselves. All this brought them together, and ended the frigid isolation of the previous months.

During the afternoon Wilder played with his sons and waited for the evening to come. Helen moved silently around the apartment, barely aware of her husband. After the fit of compulsive laughter the previous evening, her face was waxy and expressionless. Now and then a tic flickered in the right apex of her mouth, as if reflecting a tremor deep within her mind. She sat at the dining-table, mechanically straightening the boys' hair. Watching her, and unable to think of what he could do to help her, Wilder almost believed that it was she who was leaving him, rather than the contrary.

As the light began to fade, Wilder watched the first of the residents return from their offices. Among them, stepping from her car, was Jane Sheridan. Six months earlier, Wilder had broken off a brief affair with the actress, ironically enough because of the effort involved in reaching the 37th floor. He had found it difficult to be himself in her apartment. All the time he was conscious of the distance to the ground, and of his wife and children far below him, deep in the lowest seams of the building like the exploited women and child labourers of the nineteenth century. Watching television during their sexual acts in her chintz-lined bedroom, he felt as if he were high over the city in a lavish executive airliner fitted with boudoir and cocktail bar. Their conversations, even their diction and vocabulary, had become as stylized as those of strangers in adjacent aircraft seats.

The actress walked to the private entrance of the upper-floor elevator lobby, picking her way casually through the broken bottles and empty cans. A single journey to her apartment would carry him, like a ladder in a board game, virtually to the top of the high-rise with one throw of the dice.

Helen was putting the boys to bed. She had moved the wardrobe and dressing-table around their beds, in an attempt to shield them from the noise and disturbances which the night would bring.

'Richard ...? Are you going ...?'

As she spoke she emerged briefly from the deep well inside herself, aware for these few seconds that she and her sons were about to be left on their own.

Wilder waited for this moment of lucidity to pass, knowing that it would be impossible to describe his self-imposed mission to Helen. She sat silently on her bed, a hand resting on the pile of children's books, watching him in the mirror with an unchanging expression as he stepped into the corridor.

Wilder soon found that it was more difficult than he had assumed to climb to the 37th floor. The five top-floor elevators were either out of order or had been taken to the upper levels and parked there with their doors jammed open. The 2nd-floor lobby was crowded with Wilder's neighbours, some in office suits, others in beach wear, arguing with each other like disgruntled tourists caught by a currency crisis. Wilder pushed through them to the staircase, and began the long climb to the 10th floor, where he stood a better chance of finding an ascending elevator.

When he reached the 5th floor he met the dozen members of the airline pilots' raiding party returning from another of their abortive missions. Angry and shaken, they shouted at the people jeering down at them from the stairwell above. The entrance to the 10th-floor concourse had been blocked by desks and chairs taken from the junior school and flung down the stairs. The raiding party, made up of parents of the children attending the school, had tried to replace the desks, harassed by residents from the middle floors waiting impatiently for the liquor store to be re-stocked.

Wilder pressed on past them. By the time he reached the 10th floor the opposing group had moved off in a posse. Wilder stepped over the broken desks lying on the steps, pencils and crayons scattered around them. Wishing that he had brought his camera with him, he noticed two 18th-floor residents, a chemical engineer and a personnel manager, standing by the door. Each had a cine-camera and was carefully filming the scene below, following Wilder as he climbed towards them.

Leaving them to complete these dubious private newsreels, Wilder pushed back the swing doors, and looked out at the deck of the shopping mall. Hundreds of residents jostled against each other, pulling and shoving among the wine-bins and shelves of detergent packs, wire trollies locked together in a mesh of chromium wire. Voices rose in anger above the singing of the cash registers. Meanwhile, as these scuffles took place, a line of women customers sat under the driers in the hairdressing salon, calmly reading their magazines. The two cashiers on evening duty at the bank impassively counted out their bank-notes.

Giving up any attempt to cross the concourse, Wilder turned into the deserted swimming-pool. The water level was down by at least six inches, as if someone had been stealing the yellowing fluid. Wilder walked around the pool. An empty wine bottle floated in the centre, surrounded by a swill of cigarette packs and unravelling cigar butts. Below the diving-boards a newspaper hung slackly in the water, its wavering headline like a message from another world.

In the 10th-floor lobby a crowd of residents pressed impatiently against the elevator doors, their arms laden with liquor cartons and delicatessen purchases, raw materials for the aggressive parties of that evening. Wilder returned to the staircase. Somewhere above him these passengers would step out of their elevators and give him a chance to get aboard.

He climbed the steps two at a time. The staircase was deserted – the higher up the building the more reluctant were the residents to use the stairs, as if this in some way demeaned them. As he pressed on upwards Wilder peered through the windows at the car-park sinking from view below. The distant arm of the river stretched towards the darkening outline of the city, a signpost pointing towards a forgotten world.

As he turned into the final stretch of steps to the 14th floor, picking his way among the discarded cans and cigarette packs, something moved above his head. Wilder paused and looked up, his lungs pumping in the silence. A kitchen chair whirled through the air towards his head, hurled down by an assailant three floors above. Wilder flinched back as the steel chair struck the railing, glancing against his right arm before spinning away.

Wilder crouched against the steps, shielding himself below the overhang of the next floor. He massaged his bruised arm. At least three or four people were waiting for him, ostentatiously tapping their clubs on the metal railing. Fists clenching, Wilder searched the steps for a weapon. Danger in the streets of the sky – his first impulse was to rush the stairs and counter-attack.

With his powerful physique he knew that he could put to flight any three residents of the high-rise, these under-exercised and over-weight account executives and corporation lawyers egged on into this well-bred violence by their pushy wives. However, he calmed himself, deciding against a frontal attack – he would reach the top of the high-rise, but by guile rather than by brute force.

He moved down to the 13th-floor landing. Through the walls of the elevator shaft he could hear the rails and cables humming. Passengers were stepping out of the elevators on to their floors. But the doors into the 13th-floor lobby had been bolted. A face frowned out at him, a well-groomed hand curtly waved him away.

All the way down to the 10th floor the communicating doors had been locked or barricaded. Frustrated, Wilder returned to the shopping mall. A large crowd was still waiting by the elevators. They formed clearly demarked groups from different floors, each commandeering its own transit system.

Wilder left them and strode towards the supermarket. The shelves had been stripped, and the staff had left after locking the turnstiles. Wilder vaulted over a check-out counter and made his way to the store-room at the rear. Beyond the pyramids of empty cartons was one of the three service cores of the high-rise, containing a freight elevator, and the water, air-conditioning and electrical supply trunks.

Wilder waited as the elevator descended cumbrously down its shaft. The size of a carrier's aircraft lift, it had been designed to carry kitchen-appliance islands, bathroom units, and the huge pop-art and abstract-expressionist paintings favoured by the residents of the high-rise.

As he pulled back the steel grille he noticed a thin-shouldered young woman hiding behind the control panel. She was pallid and undernourished, but she watched Wilder with interest, as if glad to welcome him to this private domain.

'How far do you want to go?' she asked him. 'We can travel anywhere. I'll ride with you.'

Wilder recognized her as a masseuse from the 5th floor, one of the vagrants who spent their time wandering around the high-rise, the denizens of an interior world who formed a second invisible population. 'All right – what about the 35th floor?'

'The people on the 30th are nicer.' Expertly she pressed the control buttons, activating the heavy doors. Within seconds the elevator was carrying them ponderously aloft. The young masseuse smiled at him encouragingly, alive now that they were moving. 'If you want to go higher, I'll show you. There are a lot of air-shafts, you know. The trouble is, dogs have got into them – they're getting hungry ...'

An hour later, when Wilder stepped out into the lavishly carpeted lobby of the 37th floor, he realized that he had discovered a second building inside the one that he had originally occupied. He left behind the young masseuse, endlessly climbing the service shafts and freight wells of the high-rise, transits that externalized an odyssey taking place inside her head. During his roundabout route with her – changing to a second freight elevator to climb three floors to the 28th, moving up and down a maze of corridors on the borders of hostile enclaves, until finally taking an upper-level elevator a journey of one storey – Wilder had seen the way in which the middle and upper levels of the building had organized themselves.

While his neighbours on the lower floors remained a confused rabble united only by their sense of impotence, here everyone had joined a local group of thirty adjacent apartments, informal clans spanning two or three floors based on the architecture of corridors, lobbies and elevators. There were now some twenty of these groups, each of which had formed local alliances with those on either side. There was a marked increase in vigilante activity of all kinds. Barriers were being set up, fire-doors locked, garbage thrown down the stairwells or dumped on rival landings.

On the 29th floor Wilder came across a commune composed exclusively of women, a cluster of apartments dominated by an elderly children's-story writer, a woman of intimidating physique and personality. Sharing an apartment with her were three air-hostesses from the 1st floor. Wilder walked gingerly down the corridor between their apartments, glad of the company of the young masseuse. What unsettled Wilder, as the women questioned him in pairs from their half-open doors, was their hostility to him, not only because he was a man, but because he was so obviously trying to climb to a level above their own.

He stepped out with relief into the deserted lobby of the 37th floor. He stood by the staircase doors, suspicious that no one was guarding the lobby. Conceivably the residents here were unaware of what was going on beneath their feet. The carpets in the silent corridors were thick enough to insulate them from hell itself.

He walked down the corridor towards Jane Sheridan's apartment. She might be surprised to see him, but Wilder was confident that he would spend the night with her. The next day he would move in permanently, and visit Helen and the boys on his way to and from the television studios.

As he pressed the bell he could hear her strong, masculine voice through the door, its tone familiar from countless television costume-dramas. At last the door opened, held on its latch chain. When she looked out at Wilder, recognizing him immediately, he knew that she had been waiting for him to arrive. She was detached and uneasy at the same time, like a spectator forced to watch someone about to be involved in an accident. Wilder remembered that he had given his destination to one of the women's vigilante groups.

'Jane, you're expecting me. I'm flattered.'

'Wilder … I can't—'

Before Wilder could speak the door of the next apartment opened sharply. Staring at Wilder with undisguised hostility were a tax specialist from the 40th floor and an over-muscled choreographer with whom Wilder had often heaved a medicine ball in the 10th-floor gymnasium.

Realizing that his arrival had been anticipated by all these people, Wilder turned to leave, but the corridor behind him was blocked. A group of six residents had emerged together from the elevator lobby. They wore track suits and white sneakers, and at first sight looked like a middle-aged gymnasium dumb-bell team, each carrying his polished wooden clubs. Leading this antique but spritely troupe, which consisted of a stockbroker, two paediatricians and three senior academics, was Anthony Royal. As usual he wore his white safari-jacket, a costume which always irritated Wilder, the kind of garment that might be affected by an eccentric camp-commander or zoo-keeper. The corridor lighting flushed his blond hair and picked out the scars on his forehead, a confusing notation that hung like a series of mocking question marks over his stern expression. As he approached Wilder the chromium walking-stick flicked in his hand like a cane. Wilder watched the polished shaft catch the light, looking forward with pleasure to wrapping it around Royal's neck.

Although well aware that he had been trapped, Wilder found himself laughing aloud at the sight of this lunatic troupe. When the lights failed, first dipping warningly and then going out altogether, he backed against the wall to allow the group to pass. The wooden clubs clicked around him in the darkness, beating out a well-rehearsed tattoo. From the open door of Jane Sheridan's apartment a torch flared at him.

Around Wilder the dumb-bell troupe was beginning its act. The first clubs whirled in the torch-light. Without any warning, he felt a flurry of blows on his shoulders. Before he fell Wilder seized one of the clubs, but the others struck him to the carpeted floor at Anthony Royal's feet.

When he woke he was lying outstretched on a sofa in the ground-floor entrance lobby. Fluorescent lights shone around him, reflected in the glass ceiling-panels. With their toneless glow they seemed to have been shining for ever somewhere inside his head. Two residents returning late to the high-rise waited by the elevators. Holding tightly to their briefcases, they ignored Wilder, whom they clearly assumed to be drunk.

Aware of his bruised shoulders, Wilder reached up and nursed the swollen mastoid bone behind his right ear. When he could stand, he wandered away from the sofa towards the entrance and steadied himself against the glass doors. The lines of parked cars stretched through the darkness, enough transport to evacuate him to a thousand and one destinations. He walked out into the cold night air. Holding his neck, he looked up at the face of the high-rise. He could almost pick out the lights of the 37th floor. He felt suddenly exhausted, as much by the building's weight and mass as by his own failure. His casual and unthought-out attempt to scale the building had ended humiliatingly. In a sense he had been rejected more by the high-rise than by Royal and his friends.

Lowering his eyes from the roof, he saw that his wife, fifty feet above him, was watching from the balcony of their apartment. Despite his dishevelled clothes and bruised face she showed no concern, as if she no longer recognized him.

7

PREPARATIONS FOR DEPARTURE

High above, on the 40th floor, the first two residents were preparing to leave.

All day Anthony Royal and his wife had been packing. After lunch in the deserted restaurant on the 35th floor they returned to their apartment, where Royal spent what he knew would be his last hours in the high-rise closing down his design studio. In no hurry to leave, now that the moment had come for them to abandon the building, Royal deliberately took his time over this last ritual task.

The air-conditioning had ceased to function, and the absence of its vague familiar hum – once a source of minor irritation – made Royal restless. However reluctantly, he was now forced to recognize what he had been trying to repress for the past month, despite the evidence of his eyes. This huge building he had helped to design was moribund, its vital functions fading one by one – the water-pressure falling as the pumps faltered, the electrical sub-stations on each floor switching themselves off, the elevators stranded in their shafts.

As if in sympathy, the old injuries to his legs and back had begun to keen again. Royal leaned against his drawing-stand, feeling the pain radiate upwards from his knees into his groin. Gripping the chromium cane, he left the studio and moved among the tables and armchairs in the drawing-room, each shrouded in its dust-sheet. In the year since his accident he had found that constant exercise alone held back the pain, and he missed the games of squash with Robert Laing. Like his own physicians, Laing had told him that the injuries sustained in car-crashes took a great deal of time to heal, but Royal recently had begun to suspect that these wounds were playing a devious role of their own.

The three suitcases he had packed that morning stood ready in the hall. Royal stared down at them, for a moment hoping that they belonged to someone else. The cases had never been used, and the prominent part they would soon play in his personal Dunkirk only rubbed in the humiliation.

Royal returned to the studio and continued to take down the architectural drawings and design studies pinned to the walls. This small office in a converted bedroom he had used for his work on the development project, and the collection of books and blueprints, photographs and drawing-boards, originally intended to give a sense of purpose to his convalescence, had soon become a kind of private museum. The majority of the plans and design studies had been superseded by his colleagues after the accident, but in a strange way these old frontal elevations of the concert-hall and television studios, like the photograph of himself standing on the roof of the high-rise on hand-over day, described a more real world than the building which he was now about to abandon.

The decision to leave their apartment, already postponed for too long, had been difficult to take. For all his professional identification with the high-rise as one of its architects, Royal's contribution had been minor, but sadly for him had concerned those very sections which had borne the brunt of the residents' hostility – the 10th-floor concourse, the junior school, the observation roof with its children's sculpture-garden, and the furnishing and design of the elevator lobbies. Royal had gone to immense care in the choice of wall surfaces, now covered by thousands of aerosolled obscenities. It was stupid of him, perhaps, but it was difficult not to take them personally, particularly as he was only too aware of his neighbours' hostility towards him – the chromium cane and white Alsatian were no longer theatrical props.

In principle, the mutiny of these well-to-do professional people against the building they had collectively purchased was no different from the dozens of well-documented revolts by working-class tenants against municipal tower-blocks that had taken place at frequent intervals during the post-war years. But once again Royal had found himself reacting personally to these acts of vandalism. The breakdown of the building as a social structure was a rebellion against himself, so much so that in the early days after the jeweller's unexplained death he expected to be physically attacked.

Later, however, the collapse of the high-rise began to strengthen his will to win through. The testing of the building he had helped to design was a testing of himself. Above all, he became aware that a new social order was beginning to emerge around him. Royal was certain that a rigid hierarchy of some kind was the key to the elusive success of these huge buildings. As he often pointed out to Anne, office blocks containing as many as thirty thousand workers functioned smoothly for decades thanks to a social hierarchy as rigid and as formalized as an anthill's, with an incidence of crime, social unrest, and petty misdemeanours that was virtually nil. The confused but unmistakable emergence of this new social order – apparently based on small tribal enclaves – fascinated Royal. To begin with, he had been determined to stay on, come what may and whatever the hostility directed against him, in the hope of acting as its midwife. In fact, this alone had stopped him from notifying his former colleagues of the mounting chaos within the building. As he told himself repeatedly, the present breakdown of the high-rise might well mark its success rather than its failure. Without realizing it, he had given these people a means of escaping into a new life, and a pattern of social organization that would become the paradigm of all future high-rise blocks.

But these dreams of helping the two thousand residents towards their new Jerusalem meant nothing to Anne. As the air-conditioning and electricity supply began to fail, and it became dangerous to move unaccompanied around the building, she told Royal that they were leaving. Playing on Royal's concern for her, and his own feelings of guilt about the breakdown of the high-rise, she soon persuaded him that they must go.

Curious to see how she was getting on with her packing, Royal walked into his wife's bedroom. Two wardrobe trunks, and a selection of small and large suitcases, jewellery boxes and vanity cases lay open on the floor and dressing-table like a luggage store display. Anne was packing, or unpacking, one of the cases in front of the dressing-table mirror. Recently, Royal had noticed that she deliberately surrounded herself with mirrors, as if this replication of herself gave her some kind of security. Anne had always taken for granted a naturally deferential world, and the last few weeks, even in the comparative safety of this penthouse apartment, she had found more and more trying. The childlike strains in her character had begun to come out again, as if she was suiting her behaviour to the over-extended Mad-Hatter's tea-party that she had been forced to attend like a reluctant Alice. The journey down to the 35th-floor restaurant had become a daily ordeal, and only the prospect of leaving the apartment building for good had kept her going.

She stood up and embraced Royal. As usual, without thinking, she touched the scars on his forehead with her lips, as if trying to read a digest of the twenty-five years that separated them, a key to that part of Royal's life she had never known. As he recovered from the accident, sitting in the windows of the penthouse or exercising on the callisthenics machine, he had noticed how much his wounds had intrigued her.

'What a mess.' She gazed down hopefully at the jumble of suitcases. 'I'll be about an hour – have you called the taxi?'

'We'll need at least two. They refuse to wait now – there's no point in calling them until we're on the doorstep.'

Both their own cars, parked in the line nearest the building, had been damaged by the tenants below, their windscreens knocked out by falling bottles.

Anne returned to her packing. 'The important thing is that we're going. We should have left a month ago when I wanted to. Why anyone stays on here I can't imagine.'

'Anne, we're *leaving* …'

'At last – and why has no one called the police? Or complained to the owners?'

'We are the owners.' Royal turned his head away from her, his smile of affection stiffening. Through the windows he watched the light fading across the curtain-walling of the nearby high-rises. Inevitably, he had always taken Anne's criticisms as a comment on himself.

As Royal knew now, his young wife would never be happy in the special atmosphere of the high-rise. The only daughter of a provincial industrialist, she had been brought up in the insulated world of a large country house, a finicky copy of a

Loire chateau maintained by a staff of servants in the full-blown nineteenth-century manner. In the apartment building, by contrast, the servants who waited on her were an invisible army of thermostats and humidity sensors, computerized elevator route-switches and over-riders, playing their parts in a far more sophisticated and abstract version of the master-servant relationship. However, in Anne's world it was not only necessary for work to be done, but be seen to be done. The steady breakdown of the building's services, and the confrontation between the rival groups of tenants, had been too much for her, playing on her huge sense of insecurity, all her long-ingrained upper-class uncertainties about maintaining her superior place in the world. The present troubles in the apartment block had exposed these mercilessly. When he had first met her, Royal had taken for granted her absolute self-confidence, but in fact the reverse was true – far from being sure of herself, Anne needed constantly to re-establish her position on the top rung of the ladder. By comparison, the professional people around her, who had achieved everything as a result of their own talents, were models of self-assurance.

When they first moved into the high-rise as its first tenants, they had both intended the apartment to be no more than a *pied à terre*, conveniently close to Royal's work on the development project. As soon as they found a house in London they would leave. But Royal noticed that he continued to postpone any decision to move out. He was intrigued by life in this vertical township, and by the kind of people attracted to its smooth functionalism. As the first tenant, and owner of the best and highest apartment, he felt himself to be lord of the manor – borrowing a phrase he disliked from Anne's rule book. His sense of physical superiority as a sometime amateur tennis champion – a minor hard-courts title, though no less impressive for that – had inevitably slackened with the passage of years, but in a way had been rekindled by the presence of so many people directly below him, on the shoulders of whose far more modest dwellings his own rested securely.

Even after his accident, when he had been forced to sell out his partnership and retreat to a wheelchair in the penthouse, he had felt this sense of renewed physical authority. During the months of convalescence, as his wounds healed and his body grew stronger, each of the new tenants in some way seemed identified with his strengthening muscles and sinews, his quickening reflexes, each one bringing his invisible tribute to Royal's well-being.

For Anne, by contrast, the continued flow of new arrivals puzzled and irritated her. She had enjoyed the apartment when they were alone in the high-rise, taking it for granted that no one else would appear. She rode the elevators as if they were the grandly upholstered gondolas of a private funicular, swam alone in the undisturbed waters of the two swimming-pools, and strolled about the shopping concourse as if visiting her own personal bank, hairdresser and supermarket. By the time that the last of the two thousand residents had appeared and taken their place below, Anne was impatient to move.

But Royal was drawn to his new neighbours, exemplars beyond anything he had previously imagined of the puritan work ethic. In turn, he knew from Anne that his neighbours found him a puzzling and aloof figure, an automobile-crash casualty in his wheelchair living on the roof of the high-rise in a casual ménage with a rich young wife half his age whom he was happy to see taken out by other men. Despite this symbolic emasculation, Royal was still regarded in some way as having the key to the building. His scarred forehead and chromium cane, the white jacket which he affected and wore like a target, together seemed to be the elements of a code that concealed the real relationship between the architect of this huge building and its uneasy tenants. Even Anne's always imminent promiscuities were part of this same system of ironies, appealing to Royal's liking for the 'game' situation where one could risk everything and lose nothing.

The effect of all this on his neighbours interested Royal, and particularly on those mavericks such as Richard Wilder, who would set out to climb Everest equipped with nothing more than a sense of irritation that the mountain was larger than himself, or Dr Laing, staring out all day from his balcony under the fond impression that he was totally detached from the high-rise, when in fact he was probably its most true tenant. At least Laing knew his place and kept to it; three nights earlier they had been forced to give Wilder a short sharp lesson.

Thinking about Wilder's intrusion – only one in a series of attempts by people below to break into the top-floor apartments – Royal left the bedroom and checked the bolts on the front door.

Anne waited while he stood in the deserted corridor. There was a continuous sullen murmur from the lower levels carried up the elevator shafts. She pointed to Royal's three suitcases.

'Is that all you're taking?'

'For the time being. I'll come back for anything else.'

'Come back? Why should you want to? Perhaps you'd rather stay?'

To himself, rather than to his wife, Royal remarked, 'First to arrive, last to leave …'

'Is that a joke?'

'Of *course* not.'

Anne placed a hand on his chest, as if searching for an old wound. 'It's really all over, you know. I hate to say it, but this place hasn't worked.'

'Perhaps not …' Royal took her commiseration with a strong dose of salt. Without realizing it, Anne often played on his sense of failure, frightened by Royal's new resolve to prove himself, this conviction that the building might succeed after all. In addition, their neighbours had accepted him a little too readily as their leader. His partnership in the consortium had been largely paid for by the commissions her father had steered his way, a fact Anne had never let him forget, not to humble

Royal so much as to prove her own value to him. The point was made, though. He had come up in the world, all right, in too many senses of the term. In an insane way, his accident might have been an attempt to break out of the trap.

But all this belonged to the past now. As Royal knew, they were leaving just in time. During the last few days life in the high-rise had become impossible. For the first time the top-floor residents were directly involved. The erosion of everything continued, a slow psychological avalanche that was carrying them downwards.

Superficially, life in the apartment building was normal enough – most of the residents left for their offices each day, the supermarket was still open, the bank and hairdressing salon functioned as usual. None the less, the real internal atmosphere was that of three uneasily coexisting armed camps. A complete hardening of positions had taken place, and there was now almost no contact between the upper, middle and lower groups. During the early part of the day it was possible to move freely around the building, but as the afternoon proceeded this became increasingly difficult. By dusk any movement was impossible. The bank and supermarket closed at three o'clock. The junior school had moved from its vandalized classrooms to two apartments on the 7th floor. Few children were ever seen above the 10th floor, let alone in the sculpture-garden on the roof which Royal had designed for them with so much care. The 10th-floor swimming-pool was a half-empty pit of yellowing water and floating debris. One of the squash courts had been locked, and the other three were filled with garbage and broken classroom furniture. Of the twenty elevators in the building, three were permanently out of order, and by evening the remainder had become the private transit lines of the rival groups who could seize them. Five floors were without electricity. At night the dark bands stretched across the face of the high-rise like dead strata in a fading brain.

Fortunately for Royal and his neighbours, conditions in the upper section of the building had yet to decline so steeply. The restaurant had discontinued its evening service, but a limited luncheon was available each day during the few hours when the small staff could freely enter and leave. However, the two waiters had already gone, and Royal guessed that the chef and his wife would soon follow. The swimming-pool on the 35th floor was usable, but the level had fallen, and the water supply, like that to their own apartment, was dependent on the vagaries of the roof tanks and electric pumps.

From the drawing-room windows Royal looked down into the parking-lot. Many of the cars had not been moved for weeks – windscreens broken by falling bottles, cabins filled with garbage, they sat on flattening tyres, surrounded by a sea of rubbish that spread outwards around the building like an enlarging stain.

This visible index of the block's decline at the same time measured the extent to which its tenants accepted this process of erosion. At times Royal suspected that his neighbours unconsciously hoped that everything would decline even further. Royal had noticed that the manager's office was no longer besieged by indignant residents. Even his own top-floor neighbours, who in the early days had been only too quick to complain about everything, now never criticized the building. In the absence of the manager – still lying in a state of mental collapse in his ground-floor apartment – his dwindling staff of two (the wives of a dubbing-mixer on the 2nd floor and a first violinist on the 3rd) sat stoically at their desks in the entrance lobby, oblivious of the deterioration going on apace over their heads.

What interested Royal was the way in which the residents had become exaggeratedly crude in their response to the apartment building, deliberately abusing the elevators and air-conditioning systems, over-straining the power supply. This carelessness about their own convenience reflected a shuffling of mental priorities, and perhaps the emergence of the new social and psychological order for which Royal was waiting. He remembered the attack on Wilder, who had laughed happily as the group of paediatricians and academics had flailed away at him with their dumb-bells like a troupe of demented gymnasts. Royal had found the episode grotesque, but he guessed that in some obscure way Wilder had been glad to be flung half-conscious into an elevator.

Royal strolled around the shrouded furniture. He raised his stick and slashed at the stale air with the same stroke he had used against Wilder. At any moment a battalion of police would arrive and cart them all off to the nearest jail. Or would they? What played straight into the residents' hands was the remarkably self-contained nature of the high-rise, a self-administered enclave within the larger private domain of the development project. The manager and his staff, the personnel who manned the supermarket, bank and hairdressing salon, were all residents of the apartment building; the few outsiders had left or been sacked. The engineers who serviced the building did so on instructions from the manager, and clearly none had been issued. They might even have been told to stay away – no garbage-collection vehicle had called for several days, and a large number of the chutes were blocked.

Despite the growing chaos around them, the residents showed less interest in the external world. Bales of unsorted mail lay about in the ground-floor lobbies. As for the debris scattered around the high-rise, the broken bottles and cans, these were barely noticeable from the ground. Even the damaged cars were to some extent concealed by the piles of building materials, wooden forms and sand-pits that had yet to be cleared away. Besides, as part of that unconscious conspiracy to shut out the external world, no visitors came to the high-rise. He and Anne had invited none of their friends to the apartment for months.

Royal watched his wife move about vaguely in her bedroom. Jane Sheridan, Anne's closest friend, had called and was helping her to pack. The two women were transferring a line of evening gowns from the wardrobe racks to the trunks, and at the same time returning unwanted shirts and trousers from the suitcases back to the shelves. For all the activity it was uncertain whether they were packing on the eve of departure or unpacking on arrival.

'Anne – are you coming or going?' Royal asked. 'We hardly stand a chance of making it tonight.'

Anne gestured helplessly at the half-filled cases. 'It's the air-conditioning – I can't think.'

'You won't get out now even if you want to,' Jane told her. 'We're marooned here, as far as I can see. All the elevators have been commandeered by other floors.'

'What? Did you hear that?' Anne stared angrily at Royal, as if his faulty design of the elevator lobbies was directly responsible for these acts of piracy. 'All right, we'll leave first thing tomorrow. What about food? The restaurant will be shut.'

They had never eaten in the apartment – Anne's gesture of contempt for her neighbours' endless preparation of elaborate meals. The only food in the refrigerator was the dog's.

Royal stared at himself in the mirror, adjusting his white jacket. In the fading light his reflection had an almost spectral vibrancy, making him look like an illuminated corpse. 'We'll think of something.' A curious answer, he realized, implying that there were other sources of food than the supermarket. He looked down at Jane Sheridan's plump figure. Seeing Royal's subdued expression, she was smiling reassuringly at him. Royal had taken on the task of looking after this amiable young woman since the death of her Afghan.

'The elevators may be free in an hour or so,' he told them. 'We'll go down to the supermarket.' Thinking of the Alsatian – presumably asleep on his bed in the penthouse – he decided to exercise it on the roof.

Anne had begun to empty the half-filled suitcases. She seemed barely aware of what she was doing, as if a large part of her mind had been switched off. For all her complaints, she had never telephoned the building manager herself. Perhaps she felt this was beneath her, but nor had she mentioned the smallest criticism to any of their friends in the world beyond the apartment building.

Thinking about this, Royal noticed that the plug of her bedside telephone had been pulled from its socket, and the cable neatly wrapped around the receiver.

As he walked around the apartment before going to search for the dog, he saw that the three other external telephones, in the hall, drawing-room and kitchen, had also been disconnected. Royal realized why they had received no outside calls during the previous week, and felt a distinct sense of security at knowing that they would receive none in the future. Already he guessed that, for all their expressed intentions, they would not be leaving either the following morning or any other …

8

THE PREDATORY BIRDS

From the open windows of the penthouse Royal watched the huge birds clustering on the elevator heads fifty feet away. An unfamiliar species of estuarine gull, they had come up the river during the previous months and begun to congregate among the ventilation shafts and water storage tanks, infesting the tunnels of the deserted sculpture-garden. During his convalescence he had watched them arrive as he sat in his wheelchair on the private terrace. Later, when the callisthenics machine had been installed, the birds would hobble around the terrace while he exercised. In some way they were attracted by Royal's white jacket and pale hair, so close in tone to their own vivid plumage. Perhaps they identified him as one of their own, a crippled old albatross who had taken refuge on this remote roof-top beside the river? Royal liked this notion and often thought about it.

The french windows swung in the early evening air. The Alsatian had escaped, hunting by itself on the five-hundred-feet-long observation deck. Now that the summer had ended few people went up to the roof. The remains of a cocktail-party marquee, bedraggled in the rain, lay in the gutter below the balustrade. The gulls, heavy wings folded, strutted among the cheese sticks scattered around a cardboard carton. The potted palms had been untended for months, and the whole roof increasingly resembled a voracious garden.

Royal stepped down on to the roof deck. He enjoyed the hostile gaze of the birds sitting on the elevator heads. The sense of a renascent barbarism hung among the overturned chairs and straggling palms, the discarded pair of diamanté sunglasses from which the jewels had been picked. What attracted the birds to this isolated realm on the roof? As Royal approached, a group of the gulls dived into the air, soaring down to catch the scraps flung from a balcony ten floors below them. They fed on the refuse thrown into the car-park, but Royal liked to think that their real motives for taking over the roof were close to his own, and that they had flown here from some archaic landscape, responding to the same image of the sacred violence to come. Fearing that they might leave, he frequently brought them food, as if to convince them that the wait would be worth their while.

He pushed back the rusty gates of the sculpture-garden. From the casement of a decorative lantern he took out a box of cereal meal, by rights reserved for the Alsatian. Royal began to scatter the grains among the concrete tunnels and geometric forms of the play-sculptures. Designing the garden had given him particular satisfaction, and he was sorry that the children no longer used the playground. At least it was open to the birds. The gulls followed him eagerly, their strong wings almost knocking the cereal box from his hands.

Leaning on his stick, Royal swung himself around the pools of water on the concrete floor. He had always wanted his own zoo, with half a dozen large cats and, more important, an immense aviary stocked with every species of bird. Over the years he had sketched many designs for the zoo, one of them – ironically – a high-rise structure, where the birds would be free to move about in those sections of the sky that were their true home. Zoos, and the architecture of large structures, had always been Royal's particular interest.

The drenched body of a Siamese cat lay in the gutter where the birds had cornered it – the small beast had climbed all the way up a ventilation shaft from the warm comfort of an apartment far below, embracing the daylight for a few last seconds before the birds destroyed it. Next to the cat was the carcass of a dead gull. Royal picked it up, surprised by its weight, stepped forward and with a powerful running throw hurled the bird far out into the air. It plummeted towards the ground, in an almost unending downward plunge, until it burst like a white bomb across the bonnet of a parked car.

No one had seen him, but Royal would not have cared anyway. For all his keen interest in his neighbours' behaviour, he found it difficult not to look down on them. The five years of his marriage to Anne had given him a new set of prejudices. Reluctantly, he knew that he despised his fellow residents for the way in which they fitted so willingly into their appointed slots in the apartment building, for their over-developed sense of responsibility, and lack of flamboyance.

Above all, he looked down on them for their good taste. The building was a monument to good taste, to the well-designed kitchen, to sophisticated utensils and fabrics, to elegant and never ostentatious furnishings – in short, to that whole aesthetic sensibility which these well-educated professional people had inherited from all the schools of industrial design, all the award-winning schemes of interior decoration institutionalized by the last quarter of the twentieth century. Royal detested this orthodoxy of the intelligent. Visiting his neighbours' apartments, he would find himself physically repelled by the contours of an award-winning coffee-pot, by the well-modulated colour schemes, by the good taste and intelligence that, Midas-like, had transformed everything in these apartments into an ideal marriage of function and design. In a sense, these people were the vanguard of a well-to-do and well-educated proletariat of the future, boxed up in these expensive apartments with their elegant furniture and intelligent sensibilities, and no possibility of escape. Royal would have given anything for one vulgar mantelpiece ornament, one less than snow-white lavatory bowl, one hint of hope. Thank God that they were at last breaking out of this fur-lined prison.

*

On either side of him, the rain-soaked concrete stretched away into the evening mist. There were no signs of the white Alsatian. Royal had reached the centre of the roof. The gulls sat on the ventilation shafts and elevator heads, watching him with their unusually alert eyes. Thinking that they might already have dined off the dog, Royal kicked aside an over-turned chair and set off towards the stairhead, calling out the Alsatian's name.

Ten feet from the private terrace at the southern end of the roof, a middle-aged woman in a long fur coat stood by the balustrade. Shivering continuously, she stared out across the development project at the silver back of the river. A trio of lighters followed a tug upstream, and a police patrol boat cruised along the north bank.

As Royal approached he recognized the widow of the dead jeweller. Was she waiting for the police to arrive, in some perverse way too proud to call them herself? He was about to ask if she had seen the Alsatian, but he knew already that she would not reply. Her face was immaculately made up, but an expression of extreme hostility came through the rouge and powder, a gaze as hard as pain. Royal held tight to his cane. The woman's hands were hidden from sight, and he almost believed that inside the coat her jewelled fingers held a pair of unsheathed knives. For some reason he was suddenly convinced that she had been responsible for her husband's death, and that at any moment she would seize him and wrestle him over the ledge. At the same time, to his surprise, he found himself wanting to touch her, to put his arm around her shoulders. Some kind of wayward sexuality was at work. For a grotesque moment he was tempted to expose himself to her.

'I'm looking for Anne's Alsatian,' he said lamely. When she made no reply he added, 'We've decided to stay on.'

Confused by his response to this grieving woman, Royal turned away and made his way down the staircase to the floor below. Despite the pain in his legs he walked swiftly along the corridor, striking at the walls with his cane.

When he reached the central lobby the sounds of the Alsatian's frantic barking rose clearly up the nearest of the five high-speed elevator shafts. Royal pressed his head to the door panel. The elevator car, with the Alsatian snarling and leaping inside it, was on the 15th-floor, its doors jammed open. Royal could hear the heavy blows of a metal club striking at the floor and walls, and the shouts of three attackers – one of them a woman – as they beat the animal to the floor.

When the dog's yelping subsided, the elevator at last responded to the call button. The car climbed to the top floor, where the doors opened on the barely conscious dog dragging itself around the bloodied floor. The animal's head and shoulders were heavy with blood. Matted hair streaked the walls of the cabin.

Royal tried to reassure it, but the Alsatian snapped at his hand, frightened of the stick. Several of his neighbours gathered around, carrying an assortment of weapons – tennis rackets, dumb-bells and walking sticks. They were beckoned aside by a friend of Royal's, a gynaecologist named Pangbourne who lived in the apartment next to the lobby. A swimming partner of Anne's, he often played with the dog on the roof.

'Let me have a look at him … Poor devil, those savages have abused you …' Deftly he insinuated himself into the elevator and began to soothe the dog. 'We'll get him back to your apartment, Royal. Then I suggest we discuss the elevator position.'

Pangbourne knelt down on the floor, whistling a strange series of sounds at the dog. For some weeks the gynaecologist had been urging Royal to interfere with the building's electrical switching systems, as a means of retaliating against the lower floors. This supposed power over the high-rise was the chief source of Royal's authority with his neighbours, though he suspected that Pangbourne for one was well aware that he would never make use of it. With his soft hands and consulting-room manner the gynaecologist unsettled Royal slightly, as if he were always just about to ease an unwary patient into a compromising obstetric position – in fact, though, Pangbourne belonged to the new generation of gynaecologists who never actually touched their patients, let alone delivered a child. His speciality was the computerized analysis of recorded birth-cries, from which he could diagnose an infinity of complaints to come. He played with these tapes like an earlier generation of sorcerer examining the patterns of entrails. Characteristically, Pangbourne's one affair in the high-rise had been with a laboratory researcher on the 2nd floor, a slim, silent brunette who probably spent all her time tormenting small mammals. He had broken this off soon after the outbreak of hostilities.

None the less, he had a way with the injured Alsatian. Royal waited while he calmed the dog and examined its wounds. He held its muzzle in his white hands as if he had just freed the poor beast from its caul. Together, he and Royal half-carried and half-dragged the dog back to Royal's apartment.

Fortunately, Anne and Jane Sheridan had left for the 10th-floor supermarket, picking up the one elevator released for general traffic.

Pangbourne settled the dog on the dust-sheet covering one of the sofas.

'I'm glad you were here,' Royal told him. 'You're not at your practice?'

Pangbourne stroked the Alsatian's swollen head, his white hands delicate with blood. 'I attend my consultancy two mornings a week, just enough time for me to listen to the latest recordings. Otherwise I'm on guard duty here.' He peered pointedly at Royal. 'If I were you, I'd keep a closer eye on Anne – unless you want her to be …'

'Sound advice. You've never thought of leaving? The conditions now …'

The gynaecologist frowned at Royal as if unsure whether he was serious. 'I've only just moved here. Why should I concede anything to these people?' He pointed expressively at the floor with a bloodstained finger.

Impressed by the determination of this refined and punctilious man to defend his terrain, Royal followed him to the door, thanking him for his help and promising to discuss with him the sabotage of the elevators. For the next half an hour Royal cleaned the wounds of the Alsatian. Although the dog began to sleep, the bloodstains on the white dust-sheet made Royal feel increasingly restless. The assault had released in him a more than half-conscious wish for conflict. To date he had been a moderating influence, restraining his neighbours from any unnecessary retaliatory action. Now he wanted trouble at any price.

Somewhere below a falling bottle burst on a balcony, a brief explosion against the rising background of over-noisy record-players, shouts and hammering. The light in the apartment had begun to fade, the shrouded furniture suspended around him like under-inflated clouds. The afternoon had passed, and soon the danger period would begin. Thinking of Anne trying to make her way back from the 10th floor, Royal turned to leave the apartment.

By the door he stopped, holding one hand over the dial of his wrist-watch. His concern for Anne was as strong as ever – if anything he felt more possessive towards her – but he decided to let another half-hour elapse before he went in search of her. Perversely, this would increase the element of danger, the chance of confrontation. He walked calmly around the apartment, noting the telephones on the floor and the neatly wrapped cables. Even if she were trapped somewhere, Anne would be unable to call him.

While he waited for the darkness, Royal went up to the penthouse and watched the gulls on the elevator heads. In the evening light their plumage was a vibrant white. Like birds at dusk waiting among the cornices of a mausoleum, they flicked their wings against the bone-like concrete. As if agitated by Royal's confused state, they rose excitedly into the air. Royal was thinking of his wife, of the possible assaults on her, an almost sexual fever of hazard and revenge tightening his nerves. In another twenty minutes he would leave the apartment and make his killing drop down the shafts of the high-rise, murder descending. He wished he could take the birds with him. He could see them diving down the elevator shafts, spiralling through the stairwells to swoop into the corridors. He watched them wheel through the air, listening to their cries as he thought of the violence to come.

9

INTO THE DROP ZONE

At seven o'clock Anthony Royal set out with the white Alsatian to find his wife. The dog had recovered sufficiently from its beating to limp along in front of him. Its damp pelt was marked with a vivid crimson bloom. Like the bloodstains on his white jacket, Royal was proud of these signs of combat. As if mimicking the dog, he wore its blood on his chest and hips, the insignia of an executioner's apparel yet to be designed.

He began his descent into the lower depths of the building in the high-speed elevator lobby. A group of excited neighbours had just emerged from one of the cars. Four floors down, an apartment had been ransacked by a party of tenants from the 15th floor. These sporadic raids on apartments were taking place with increasing frequency. Empty apartments, even if left for no more than a single day, were especially vulnerable. Some unconscious system of communication alerted any would-be raiders that an apartment a dozen floors above or below was ripe for ransack.

With difficulty Royal found an elevator to take him down to the 35th floor. The restaurant had closed. After serving a last lunch to the Royals the chef and his wife had left for good. Chairs and tables had been stacked around the kitchen in a barricade, and the revolving door was padlocked. The long observation windows, with their magnificent view, were shuttered and chained, throwing the north end of the pool into darkness.

The last swimmer, a market analyst from the 38th floor, was leaving the swimming-pool. His wife waited protectively outside his cubicle as he changed. She watched the Alsatian lapping at the water lying on the greasy tiles by the diving-board. When the dog relieved itself against the door of an empty cubicle her face was expressionless. Royal felt a modest pride in this act, which rekindled a primitive territorial reflex. The marking of this cubicle with the dog's over-bright urine defined the small terrain coming under his sway.

For the next hour Royal continued his search for his wife, descending deeper into the central mass of the high-rise. As he moved from one floor to the next, from one elevator to another, he realized the full extent of its deterioration. The residents' rebellion against the apartment building was now in full swing. Garbage lay heaped around the jammed disposal chutes. The stairways were littered with broken glass, splintered kitchen chairs and sections of handrail. Even more significant, the pay-phones in the elevator lobbies had been ripped out, as if the tenants, like Anne and himself, had agreed to shut off any contact with the world outside.

The further down Royal reached, the greater the damage. Fire safety doors leaned off their hinges, quartz inspection windows punched out. Few corridor and staircase lights still worked, and no effort had been made to replace the broken bulbs. By eight o'clock little light reached the corridors, which became dim tunnels strewn with garbage sacks. The lurid outlines of lettered slogans, aerosolled in luminous paint across the walls, unravelled around him like the decor of a nightmare.

Rival groups of residents stood around in the lobbies, guarding their elevators and watching each other along the corridors. Many of the women had portable radios slung from their shoulders, which they switched from station to station as if tuning up for an acoustic war. Others carried cameras and flash equipment, ready to record any acts of hostility, any incursions into their territory.

By changing elevators and making journeys of two floors at a time, Royal finally descended into the lower half of the apartment building. He was unmolested by the other residents, who watched him as he entered their lobbies, moving out of his way as he strolled past. The wounded Alsatian and Royal's bloodstained jacket gave him free passage through these rival clans, as if he were a betrayed landowner descending from his keep to parade his wounds among his rebellious tenants.

By the time he reached the 10th floor the concourse was almost deserted. A few residents wandered around the shopping mall, staring at the empty chromium counters. The bank and liquor store were closed, their grilles chained. There was no sign of Anne. Royal led the Alsatian through the swing doors into the swimming-pool, now barely half full. The yellow water was filled with debris, the floor at the shallow end emerging like a beach in a garbage lagoon. A mattress floated among the bottles, surrounded by a swill of cardboard cartons and newspapers.

Even a corpse would go unnoticed here, Royal reflected. As the Alsatian snuffled its way along the vandalized changing cubicles, Royal waved his cane at the humid air, trying to stir it into life. He would soon suffocate here in the lower section of the apartment building. During even this brief visit he had felt crushed by the pressure of all the people above him, by the thousands of individual lives, each with its pent-up time and space.

From the elevator lobby on the far side of the swimming-pool came the sounds of shouting. Urging on the dog, Royal strode to the rear exit behind the diving-boards. Through the glass doors he watched a heated argument taking place outside the entrance to the junior school. Some twenty men and women were involved, one group from the lower floors carrying desks and chairs, a blackboard and artist's easel, the other trying to prevent them from re-occupying the classrooms.

Scuffles soon broke out. Egged on by a film-editor wielding a desk over his head, the parents pressed forward determinedly. Their opponents, residents from the 11th and 12th floors, stood their ground, forming a heavy-breathing cordon. A bad-tempered brawl developed, men and women wrestling clumsily with each other.

Royal pulled the Alsatian away, deciding to leave this jostling group to settle their own dispute. As he turned to continue his search for Anne, the staircase doors leading into the lobby were flung back. A group of residents, all from the 14th and 15th floors, leapt out and hurled themselves into the mêlée. They were led by Richard Wilder, cine-camera gripped like a battle standard in one hand. Royal assumed that Wilder was filming an episode from the documentary he had been talking about for so long, and had set up the entire scene. But Wilder was in the thick of the fray, aggressively wielding the cine-camera as he urged on his new allies against his former neighbours. The raiding party was shouldered back towards the staircase in disarray, the parents dropping the desks and blackboard.

Wilder slammed the staircase doors behind them. Expelling his sometime neighbours and friends had clearly given him enormous satisfaction. Waving his camera, he pointed to the classroom of the junior school. Two young women, Royal's wife and Jane Sheridan, were crouching behind an overturned desk. Like children caught red-handed in some mischief, they watched Wilder as he beckoned theatrically towards them.

Holding the Alsatian on a short leash, Royal pushed back the glass doors. He strode through the residents in the lobby, who were now happily breaking up the children's desks.

'It's all right, Wilder,' he called out in a firm but casual voice. 'I'll take over.'

He stepped past Wilder and entered the classroom. He lifted Anne to her feet. 'I'll get you out of here – don't worry about Wilder.'

'I'm not …' For all her ordeal, Anne was remarkably unruffled. She gazed at Wilder with evident admiration. 'My God, he's rather insane …'

Royal waited for Wilder to attack him. Despite the twenty years between them, he felt calm and self-controlled, ready for the physical confrontation. But Wilder made no attempt to move. He watched Royal with interest, patting one armpit in an almost animal way, as if glad to see Royal here on the lower levels, directly involved at last in the struggle for territory and womenfolk. His shirt was open to the waist, exposing a barrel-like chest that he showed off with some pride. He held the cine-camera against his cheek as if he were visualizing the setting and choreography of a complex duel to be fought at some more convenient time on a stage higher in the building.

That night, when they had returned to their apartment on the 40th floor, Royal set about asserting his leadership of the topmost levels of the high-rise. First, while his wife and Jane

Sheridan rested together in Anne's bed, Royal attended to the Alsatian. He fed the dog in the kitchen with the last of its food. The wounds on its shoulders and head were as hard as coins. Royal was more aroused by the injuries to the dog than by any indignity suffered by his wife. He had almost made Anne's ordeal certain by deliberately postponing his search for her. As he expected, she and Jane had been unable to find an elevator when they had finished shopping at the supermarket. After being molested in the lobby by a drunken sound-man they had taken refuge in the deserted classroom.

'They're all making their own films down there,' Anne told him, clearly fascinated by her heady experience of the lower orders at work and play. 'Every time someone gets beaten up about ten cameras are shooting away.'

'They're showing them in the projection theatre,' Jane confirmed. 'Crammed in there together seeing each other's rushes.'

'Except for Wilder. He's waiting for something really gruesome.'

Both women turned without thinking to look at Royal, but he took this in his stride. In an obscure way, it was his affection for Anne that had led him to display her to his neighbours below, his contribution to the new realm they would create together. By contrast, the Alsatian belonged to a more practical world. Already he knew that the dog might well prove useful, be more easily bartered than any woman, in the future that lay ahead. He decided not to throw away the bloodstained jacket, glad to wear the dog's blood against his chest. He refused any offers to clean it from the wives of his fellow residents who came in to comfort the two young women.

The assaults on the Alsatian, and on Royal's wife, made his apartment a natural focus of his neighbours' decision to regain the initiative before they were trapped on the roof of the high-rise. To Pangbourne he explained that it was vital for them to enlist the support of the tenants living on the floors immediately below the 35th.

'To survive, we need allies as a buffer against any attacks from the lower levels, and also to give us access to more of the elevators. We're in danger of being cut off from the central mass of the building.'

'Right,' the gynaecologist agreed, glad to see that Royal had at last woken up to the realities of their position. 'Once we've gained a foothold there we can play these people off against those lower down – in short balkanize the centre section and then begin the colonization of the entire building …'

In retrospect, it surprised Royal how easily they were able to implement these elementary schemes. At nine o'clock, before the evening's parties began, Royal began to enlist the support of the residents below the 35th-floor swimming-pool. Expertly, Pangbourne played on their grievances. These people shared many of the problems of the top-floor tenants – their cars had also been damaged, and they had the same struggles with the declining water-supply and air-conditioning. In a calculated gesture, Royal and Pangbourne offered them the use of the top-floor elevators. To reach their apartments they would no longer have to enter the main lobby and run the gauntlet of thirty intervening floors. They would now wait for a top-level tenant to appear, enter the private lobby with him and ride straight to the 35th floor without harassment, and then walk the few steps down to their apartments.

The offer was accepted, Royal and Pangbourne deliberately asking for no concessions in return. The deputation returned to the 40th floor, the members dispersing to their apartments to prepare for the evening's festivities. During the previous hour a few trivial incidents had occurred – the middle-aged wife of a 28th-floor account executive had been knocked unconscious into the half-empty swimming-pool, and a radiologist from the 7th floor had been beaten up among the driers in the hair-dressing salon – but in general everything within the high-rise was normal. As the night progressed, the sounds of continuous revelry filled the building. Beginning with the lower floors, the parties spread upwards through the apartment block, investing it in an armour of light and festivity. Standing on his balcony, Royal listened to the ascending music and laughter as he waited for the two young women to dress. Far below him, a car drove along the access road to the nearby high-rise, its three occupants looking up at the hundreds of crowded balconies. Anyone seeing this ship of lights would take for granted that the two thousand people on board lived together in a state of corporate euphoria.

Invigorated by this tonic atmosphere, Anne and Jane Sheridan had made a rapid recovery. Anne no longer referred to their leaving the high-rise, and seemed to have forgotten that she had ever made the decision to go. The rough and tumble in the junior school had given her that previously missing sense of solidarity with the other tenants of the high-rise. In the future, violence would clearly become a valuable form of social cement. As Royal escorted her to the first party of the evening, given by a newspaper columnist on the 37th floor, she and Jane strolled arm in arm, buoyed up by reports of further confrontations, and by the news that two more floors, the 6th and 14th, were now in darkness.

Pangbourne congratulated Royal on this, almost as if he believed that Royal was responsible. No one, even on the top floors, seemed aware of the contrast between the well-groomed revellers and the dilapidated state of the building. Along corridors strewn with uncollected garbage, past blocked disposal chutes and vandalized elevators, moved men in well-tailored dinner-jackets. Elegant women lifted long skirts to step over the debris of broken bottles. The scents of expensive after-shave lotions mingled with the aroma of kitchen wastes.

These bizarre contrasts pleased Royal, marking the extent to which these civilized and self-possessed professional men and women were moving away from any notion of rational behaviour. He thought of his own confrontation with Wilder, which summed up all the forces in collision within the high-rise.

Wilder had obviously begun his ascent of the building again, and had climbed as far as the 15th floor. By rights the high-rise should be totally deserted except for Wilder and himself. The real duel would be resolved among the deserted corridors and abandoned apartments of the building inside their heads, watched only by the birds.

Now that she had accepted it, the threat of violence in the air had matured Anne. Standing by the fireplace in the columnist's drawing-room, Royal watched her with affection. She was no longer flirting with the elderly businessmen and young entrepreneurs, but listening intently to Dr Pangbourne, as if aware that the gynaecologist might be useful to her in more ways than the purely professional. Despite his pleasure in displaying her to the other residents, Royal felt far more protective of her. This sexual territoriality extended to Jane Sheridan.

'Have you thought about moving in with us?' he asked her. 'Your own apartment is very much exposed.'

'I'd like to – Anne did mention it. I've already brought some things over.'

Royal danced with her in the garbage-stacked hallway, openly feeling her strong hips and thighs, as if this inventory established his claim to these portions of her body at a future date.

Hours later, at some period after midnight when it seemed to Royal that these parties had been going on for ever, he found himself drunk in an empty apartment on the 39th floor. He was lying back on a settee with Jane against his shoulder, surrounded by tables loaded with dirty glasses and ashtrays, all the debris of a party abandoned by its guests. The music from the balconies nearby was overlaid by the noise of sporadic acts of violence. Somewhere a group of residents was shouting in a desultory way, hammering on the doors of an elevator shaft.

A power failure had switched out the lights. Royal lay back in the darkness, steadying his slowly rotating brain against the illumination of the nearby high-rise. Without thinking, he began to caress Jane, stroking her heavy breasts. She made no attempt to pull herself away from him. A few moments later, when the electric power returned, lighting up a single table-lamp lying on the floor of the balcony, she recognized Royal and settled herself across him.

Hearing a noise from the kitchen, Royal looked round to see his wife sitting at the table in her long gown, one hand on the electric coffee-percolator as it began to warm. Royal put his arms around Jane and embraced her with deliberate slowness, as if repeating for his wife's benefit a slow-motion playback. He knew that Anne could see them, but she sat quietly at the kitchen table, lighting a cigarette. During the sexual act that followed she watched them without speaking, as if she approved, not from any fashionable response to marital infidelity, but from what Royal realized was a sense of tribal solidarity, a complete deference to the clan leader.

10

THE DRAINED LAKE

Soon after dawn the next morning, Robert Laing sat on his balcony on the 25th floor, eating a frugal breakfast and listening to the first sounds of activity in the apartments around him. Already a few residents were leaving the building on their way to work, picking their way through the debris underfoot towards their garbage-speckled cars. Several hundred people still left each day for their offices and studios, airports and auction-rooms. Despite the scarcity of water and heating, the men and women were well dressed and groomed, their appearance giving no hint of the events of the previous weeks. However, without realizing it, many of them would spend much of their time at their offices asleep at their desks.

Laing ate his slice of bread with methodical slowness. Sitting there on the cracked balcony of tiles, he felt like a poor pilgrim who had set out on a hazardous vertical journey and was performing a simple but meaningful ritual at a wayside shrine.

The previous night had brought total chaos – drunken parties, brawls, the looting of empty apartments and assaults on any isolated resident. Several more floors were now in darkness, including the 22nd, where his sister Alice lived. Hardly anyone had slept. Amazingly, few people showed any signs of fatigue, as if the economy of their lives was switching from day to night. Laing half-suspected that the insomnia so many of his neighbours had suffered had been some kind of unconscious preparation for the emergency ahead. He himself felt alert and confident – despite the bruises on his shoulders and arms, he was physically in fine trim. At eight o'clock he intended to clean himself up and leave for the medical school.

Laing had spent the early part of the night straightening Charlotte Melville's apartment, which had been ransacked by intruders while she and her small son were sheltering with friends. Later, he had helped to guard an elevator which his neighbours had seized for a few hours. Not that they had gone anywhere – having commandeered the elevator what mattered was to hold it for an effective psychological interval.

The evening had begun, as usual, with a party held by Paul Crosland, television newsreader and now clan chief. Crosland had been delayed at the studios, but his guests watched him deliver the nine-o'clock news, speaking in his familiar, well-modulated voice about a rush-hour pile-up in which six people had died. As his neighbours stood around the television set, Laing waited for Crosland to refer to the equally calamitous events taking place in the high-rise, the death of the jeweller (now totally forgotten), and the division of the tenants into rival camps. Perhaps, at the end of the newscast, he would add a special message for his clan members at that moment fixing their drinks among the plastic rubbish-sacks in his living-room.

By the time Crosland arrived, swerving into the apartment in his fleece-lined jacket and boots like a returning bomber pilot, everyone was drunk. Flushed and excited, Eleanor Powell swayed up to Laing, pointing hilariously at him and accusing him of trying to break into her apartment. Everyone cheered this news, as if rape was a valuable and well tried means of bringing clan members together.

'A low crime-rate, doctor,' she told him amiably, 'is a sure sign of social deprivation.'

Drinking steadily and without any self-control, Laing felt the alcohol bolt through his head. He knew that he was deliberately provoking himself, repressing any reservations about the good sense of people such as Crosland. On a practical level, being drunk was almost the only way of getting close to Eleanor Powell. Sober, she soon became tiresomely maudlin, wandering about the corridors in a vacant way as if she had lost the key to her own mind. After a few cocktails she was hyper-animated, and flicked on and off like a confused TV monitor revealing glimpses of extraordinary programmes which Laing could only understand when he was drunk himself. Although she kept overruling everything he said, tripping over the plastic garbage-sacks under the bar, he held her upright, excited by the play of her hands across his lapels. Not for the first time Laing reflected that he and his neighbours were eager for trouble as the most effective means of enlarging their sex lives.

Laing emptied the coffee-percolator over the edge of the balcony. A greasy spray hung across the face of the building, the residue of the cascade of debris now heaved over the side without a care whether the wind would carry it into the apartments below. He carried his breakfast tray into the kitchen. The continuing failure of the electricity supply had destroyed the food in the refrigerator. Bottles of sour milk stood in a mould-infested line. Rancid butter dripped through the grilles. The smell of this rotting food was not without its appeal, but Laing opened a plastic sack and scooped everything into it. He slung the sack into the corridor, where it lay in the dim light with a score of others.

A group of his neighbours was arguing in the elevator lobby, voices raised. A minor confrontation was developing between them and the 28th-floor residents. Crosland was bellowing aggressively into the empty elevator shaft. Usually, at this early hour of the day, Laing would have paid no attention to him. Too often Crosland had no idea what he was arguing about – confrontation was enough. Without his make-up, the expression of outrage on his face made Crosland resemble an announcer tricked for the first time into reading an item of bad news about himself.

From the shadows outside his door the orthodontic surgeon emerged with studied casualness. Steele and his hard-faced wife had been standing among the garbage-sacks for some time, keeping an eye on everything. He sidled up to Laing and took his arm in a gentle but complex grip, the kind of hold he might have used for an unusual extraction. He pointed to the floors above.

'They want to seal the doors permanently,' he explained. 'They're going to re-wire two of the elevator circuits so that they move non-stop from the ground floor to the 28th.'

'What about the rest of us?' Laing asked. 'How do we leave the building?'

'My dear Laing, I don't suppose they care very much about us. Their real intention is to divide the building in half – here, at the 25th floor. This is a key level for the electrical services. By knocking out the three floors below us they will have a buffer zone separating the top half of the building from the lower. Let's make sure, doctor, that when this happens we are on the right side of the buffers ...'

He broke off as Laing's sister approached, carrying her electric coffee-pot. With a bow, Steele moved away through the shadows, his small feet stepping deftly among the garbage sacks, the centre parting of hair gleaming in the faint light. Laing watched him slide noiselessly into his apartment. No doubt Steele would pick his way with equal skill through the hazards ahead. He never left the building now, Laing had noticed. What had happened to that ruthless ambition? After the battles of the past weeks he was presumably banking on an imminent upsurge in the demand for advanced surgery of the mouth.

As Laing greeted Alice he realized that she too would be excluded if the surgeon was right, living in the darkness on the wrong side of the dividing line with her alcoholic husband. She had come up ostensibly to plug her coffee-pot into the power point in Laing's kitchen, but when they entered the apartment she left it absently on the hall table. She walked on to the balcony and stared into the morning air, as if glad to have the three extra floors beneath her.

'How is Charles?' Laing asked. 'Is he at the office?'

'No … He's taken some leave. Terminal, if you ask me. What about you? You shouldn't neglect your students. At the present rate we're going to need every one of them.'

'I'm going in this morning. Would you like me to have a look at Charles on my way?'

Alice ignored this offer. She grasped the handrail and began to rock herself like a child. 'It's peaceful up here. Robert, you've no idea what it's like for most people.'

Laing laughed aloud, amused by Alice's notion that somehow he had been unaffected by events in the high-rise – the typical assumption of a martyred older sister forced during her childhood to look after a much younger brother.

'Come whenever you want to.' Laing put his arm around her shoulders, steadying her in case she lost her balance. In the past he had always felt physically distanced from Alice by her close resemblance to their mother, but for reasons not entirely sexual this resemblance now aroused him. He wanted to touch her hips, place his hand over her breast. As if aware of this, she leaned passively against him.

'Use my kitchen this evening,' Laing told her. 'From what I've heard, everything is going to be chaotic. You'll be safer here.'

'All right – but your apartment is so dirty.'

'I'll clean it for you.'

Checking himself, Laing looked down at his sister. Did she realize what was happening? Without intending to, they were arranging an assignation.

All over the high-rise people were packing their bags, readying themselves for short but significant journeys, a few floors up or down, laterally to the other end of a corridor. A covert but none the less substantial movement of marital partners was taking place. Charlotte Melville was now involved with a statistician on the 29th floor, and had almost vacated her apartment. Laing had watched her leave without resentment. Charlotte needed someone who would bring out her forcefulness and grit.

Thinking about her, Laing felt a pang of regret that he himself had found no one. But perhaps Alice would give him the practical support he needed, with her now unfashionable dedication to the domestic virtues. Although he disliked her shrewish manner, with its unhappy reminders of their mother, it gave him an undeniable sense of security.

Holding her shoulders, he looked up at the roof of the high-rise. It seemed months since he had last visited the observation deck, but for the first time he felt no urge to do so. He would build his dwelling-place where he was, with this woman and in this cave in the cliff face.

When his sister had gone, Laing began to prepare for his visit to the medical school. Sitting on the kitchen floor, he looked up at the unwashed plates and utensils stacked in the sink. He was leaning comfortably against a plastic sack filled with rubbish. Seeing the kitchen from this unfamiliar perspective, he realized how derelict it had become. The floor was strewn with debris, scraps of food and empty cans. To his surprise, Laing counted six garbage-sacks – for some reason he had assumed that there was only one.

Laing wiped his hands on his dirt-stained trousers and shirt. Reclining against this soft bed of his own waste, he felt like going to sleep. With an effort he roused himself. A continuous decline had been taking place for some time, a steady erosion of standards that affected not only the apartment, but his own personal habits and hygiene. To some extent this was forced on him by the intermittent water and electricity supply, the failure of the garbage-disposal system. But it also reflected a falling interest in civilized conventions of any kind. None of his neighbours cared what food they ate. Neither Laing nor his friends had prepared a decent meal for weeks, and had reached the point where they opened a can at random whenever they felt hungry. By the same token, no one cared what they drank, interested only in getting drunk as quickly as possible and blunting whatever sensibilities were left to them. Laing had not played one of his carefully built-up library of records for weeks. Even his language had begun to coarsen.

He picked at the thick rims of dirt under his nails. This decline, both of himself and his surroundings, was almost to be welcomed. In a way he was forcing himself down these steepening gradients, like someone descending into a forbidden valley. The dirt on his hands, his stale clothes and declining hygiene, his fading interest in food and drink, all helped to expose a more real vision of himself.

Laing listened to the intermittent noises from the refrigerator. The electricity had come on again, and the machine was sucking current from the mains. Water began to trickle from the taps as the pumps started to work. Spurring himself on with Alice's criticisms, Laing wandered around the apartment, doing what he could to straighten the furniture. But half an hour later, as he carried a garbage-sack from the kitchen into the hallway, he suddenly stopped. He dropped the sack on to the floor, realizing that he had achieved nothing – all he was doing was rearranging the dirt.

Far more important was the physical security of the apartment, particularly while he was away. Laing strode down the long bookcase in the sitting-room, pulling his medical and scientific text-books on to the floor. Section by section, he wrenched out the shelving. He carried the planks into the hall, and for the next hour moved around the apartment, transforming its open interior into a home-made blockhouse. All pieces of heavy furniture, the dining-table and a hand-carved oak chest in his bedroom, he pulled into the hall. With the armchairs and desk he constructed a solid barricade. When he was satisfied with this he moved his food supplies from the kitchen into the bedroom. His resources were meagre, but would keep him going for several days – bags of rice, sugar and salt, cans of beef and pork, and a stale loaf of bread.

Now that the air-conditioning had ceased, the rooms soon became stuffy. Recently Laing had noticed a strong but not unpleasant smell, the characteristic odour of the apartment – himself.

Laing stripped off his grimy sports-shirt and washed himself in the last water flowing from the shower. He shaved and put on a fresh shirt and suit. If he visited the medical school looking like a tramp he might give away to some sharp-eyed colleague what was actually going on in the high-rise. He examined himself in the wardrobe mirror. The gaunt, white-skinned figure with a bruised forehead standing awkwardly in an over-large business suit looked totally unconvincing, like a discharged convict in his release suit blinking at the unfamiliar daylight after a long prison-sentence.

After tightening the bolts on the front door, Laing let himself out of the apartment. Fortunately, leaving the high-rise was easier than moving around within it. Like an unofficial subway service, one elevator still travelled by mutual consent to and from the main entrance lobby during office hours. However, the atmosphere of tension and hostility, the complex of overlapping internal sieges, was apparent everywhere. Barricades of lobby furniture and plastic sacks filled with garbage blocked the entrances to individual floors. Not only the lobby and corridor walls, but the ceilings and carpets were covered with slogans, a jumble of coded signals that marked the attacks of raiding parties from floors above and below. Laing had to restrain himself from pencilling the number of his own floor among the numerals, some three feet high, emblazoned across the walls of the elevator car like the entries in a lunatic ledger. Almost everything possible had been vandalized – lobby mirrors fractured, pay-phones torn out, sofa upholstery slashed. The degree of vandalism was deliberately excessive, almost as if it served a more important secondary role, disguising the calculated way in which the residents of the high-rise, by ripping out all the phone lines, were cutting themselves off from the outside world.

For a few hours each day a system of informal truce routes opened like fracture lines throughout the building, but this period was becoming progressively shorter. Residents moved around the building in small groups, sharply on the lookout for any strangers. Each of them wore his floor-level on his face like a badge. During this brief armistice of four or five hours they could move about, contestants in a ritualized ladder-battle allowed between bouts to mount the rungs of their pre-ordained ranks. Laing and his fellow passengers waited as the car made its slow descent, frozen together like mannequins in a museum tableau – 'late twentieth-century high-rise dweller'.

When they reached the ground floor Laing walked cautiously through the entrance, past the shuttered manager's office and the sacks of unsorted mail. He had not been to the medical school for days, and as he stepped through the glass door he was struck immediately by the cooler light and air, like the harsh atmosphere of an alien planet. A sense of strangeness, far more palpable than anything within the building, extended around the apartment block on all sides, reaching across the concrete plazas and causeways of the development project.

Looking over his shoulder, as if maintaining a mental lifeline to the building, Laing walked across the parking-lot. Hundreds of broken bottles and cans lay among the cars. A health engineer from the central office of the project had called the previous day but left within half an hour, satisfied that these signs of breakdown were no more than teething troubles in the building's waste-disposal system. As long as the residents made no formal complaint, no action would be taken. Laing was no longer surprised by the way in which the residents, who only a few weeks earlier had been united in their anger over the breakdown of the building's services, were now just as united in assuring any outsiders that all was well – partly out of a displaced pride in the high-rise, but also out of a need to resolve the confrontation between them without interference, like rival gangs battling across a refuse tip who joined forces to expel any intruder.

Laing reached the centre of the parking-lot, only two hundred yards from the neighbouring high-rise, a sealed rectilinear planet whose glassy face he could now see clearly. Almost all the new tenants had moved into their apartments, duplicating to the last curtain fabric and dish-washer those in his own block, but this building seemed remote and threatening. Looking up at the endless tiers of balconies, he felt uneasily like a visitor to a malevolent zoo, where terraces of vertically mounted cages contained creatures of random and ferocious cruelty. A few people leaned on their railings and watched Laing without expression, and he had a sudden image of the two thousand residents springing to their balconies and hurling down at him anything to hand, inundating Laing beneath a pyramid of wine bottles and ashtrays, deodorant aerosols and contraceptive wallets.

Laing reached his car and leaned against the window pillar. He knew that he was testing himself against the excitements of the world outside, exposing himself to its hidden dangers. For all its present conflict, the high-rise represented safety and security. Feeling the warm cellulose of the window pillar against his shoulder, Laing remembered the stale air in his apartment, tepid with the smell of his own body. By comparison, the brilliant light reflected off the chromium trim of the hundreds of cars filled the air with knives.

He turned away from his car, and walked along the parking lane that ran parallel to the apartment building. He was not ready yet to venture into the open air, face his colleagues at the medical school, catch up with the lost student supervisions. Perhaps he would stay at home that afternoon and prepare his notes for his next lecture.

He reached the edge of the ornamental lake, a graceful oval two hundred yards in length, and stepped down on to the concrete floor. Following his shadow, he walked along the gently sloping lake-bed. Within a few minutes he was standing in the centre of the empty lake. The damp concrete, like the surface of an enormous mould, curved away on all sides, smooth and bland, but in some way as menacing as the contours of some deep reductive psychosis. The absence of any kind of rigid rectilinear structure summed up for Laing all the hazards of the world beyond the high-rise.

Unable to stay there any longer, he turned and strode swiftly towards the shore, climbed the bank and ran towards the apartment building between the dusty cars.

Within ten minutes he had returned to his apartment. After bolting the door, he climbed over his barricade and wandered around the half-empty rooms. As he inhaled the stale air he was refreshed by his own odour, almost recognizing parts of his body – his feet and genitalia, the medley of smells that issued from his mouth. He stripped off his clothes in the bedroom, throwing his suit and tie into the bottom of the closet and putting on again his grimy sports-shirt and trousers. He knew now that he would never again try to leave the high-rise. He was thinking about Alice, and how he could bring her to his apartment. In some way these powerful odours were beacons that would draw her to him.

11

PUNITIVE EXPEDITIONS

By four o'clock that afternoon the last of the residents had returned to the high-rise. From his balcony Laing watched their cars appear on the approach roads and turn into their spaces in the parking-lot. Briefcases in hand, the drivers made their way to the entrance lobbies. Laing was relieved that all conversation ended when they neared the building. This civilized behaviour in some way unsettled him.

Laing had rested during the afternoon, deciding to calm himself and gather his strength for the night to come. At intervals he climbed over the barricade and peered into the corridor, hoping to catch sight of Steele. Laing's concern for his sister, only three floors below with her twilight husband, made him increasingly restless. He needed an outbreak of violence to provide a pretext to rescue her. If the plan to divide the building succeeded, he would be unlikely to see her again.

Laing paced around the apartment, testing the primitive defensive preparations. Those residents like himself on the upper floors were more vulnerable than they assumed, and might easily find themselves at the mercy of those on the lower levels. Wilder and his henchmen could easily block the exits, destroy the electrical and water-supply inputs, and set fire to the upper floors. Laing imagined the first flames climbing through the elevator shafts and staircases, floors collapsing as the terrified residents were driven to find refuge on the roof.

Unsettled by this lurid vision, Laing disconnected his stereo-speakers and added them to the barricade of furniture and kitchen appliances. Records and cassettes lay about underfoot, but he kicked them out of his way. At the base of his bedroom wardrobe he prised away the floorboards. In this suitcase-sized cavity he hid away his cheque book and insurance policies, tax returns and share certificates. Lastly, he forced in his medical case with vials of morphine, antibiotics and cardiac stimulants. When he nailed the floorboards back into place he felt that he was sealing away for ever the last residues of his previous life, and preparing himself without reservation for the new one to come.

On the surface, the apartment building remained quiet, but much to Laing's relief the first incidents broke out by the early evening. He waited in the lobby through the late afternoon, standing about with a group of his fellow residents. Perhaps, insanely, *nothing* was going to happen? Then a foreign-affairs analyst arrived with the news that there had been a fierce scuffle over an elevator ten floors below. Adrian Talbot, the likeable psychiatrist on the 27th floor, had been drenched in urine as he climbed the stairs to his apartment. There was even a rumour that a 40th-floor apartment had been vandalized. Such an act of provocation guaranteed them all a hot night.

This was followed by a spate of reports that many residents had returned home to find their apartments ransacked, furniture and kitchen equipment damaged, electrical fittings torn out. Oddly enough, no food supplies had been touched, as if these acts of vandalism were deliberately random and meaningless. Had the damage been inflicted by the owners themselves, without realizing what they were doing, in an attempt to bring about an increase in violence?

These incidents continued as the evening settled over the apartment building. From his balcony Laing could see torch-beams flicking to and fro in the windows of the eight blacked-out floors below, as if signalling the preparations of a brutal blood-rite. Laing sat in the darkness on the living-room carpet, his back against the reassuring bulk of the barricade. He was reluctant to switch on the lights, for fear – absurdly, as he knew – that an assailant might attack him from the air outside his balcony. Drinking steadily from a hip-flask of whisky, he watched the early evening television programmes. He turned down the sound, not out of boredom with these documentaries and situation comedies, but because they were meaningless. Even the commercials, with their concern for the realities of everyday life, were transmissions from another planet. Squatting among the plastic garbage-sacks, his furniture piled up behind him, Laing studied these lavish reconstructions of housewives cleaning their immaculate kitchens, deodorants spraying well-groomed armpits. Together they formed the elements of a mysterious domestic universe.

Calm and unfrightened, Laing listened to the strident voices in the corridor. Thinking about his sister, he welcomed these signs of the violence to come. Alice, always fastidious, would probably be repelled by the derelict state of the apartment, but it would do her good to find something to criticize. The sweat on Laing's body, like the plaque that coated his teeth, surrounded him in an envelope of dirt and body odour, but the stench gave him confidence, the feeling that he had dominated the terrain with the products of his own body. Even the prospect that the lavatory would soon be permanently blocked, something that had once filled him with polite dread, was now almost inviting.

This decline in standards of hygiene Laing shared with his neighbours. Emitted from their bodies was a strong scent, the unique signature of the high-rise. The absence of this odour was what most unsettled him about the world outside the apartment block, though its nearest approximation was to be found in the dissecting-room at the anatomy school. A few days earlier Laing had caught himself hanging about his secretary's desk trying to get close enough to her to detect this reassuring smell. The startled girl had looked up to find Laing hovering over her like a beachcomber in rut.

*

Three floors above, a falling bottle burst across a balcony. The glass fragments spat away like tracers through the darkness. A record-player by an open window was turned up to full volume. Huge fragments of amplified music boomed into the night.

Laing climbed around his barricade and unlocked the door of his apartment. In the elevator lobby a group of his neighbours were manhandling a steel fire-door across the entrance to the stairway. Five floors below, a raid was in progress. Laing and his fellow clansmen crowded against the fire-door, peering into the darkened stairwell. They could hear the elevator gear reverberating as the car moved up and down, ferrying more attackers to the fray. Rising from the 20th floor, as if from an execution pit, came a woman's scream.

Waiting for Steele to appear and help them, Laing was about to go in search of him. But the lobby and corridors were filled with running people, colliding into each other in the dark as they fought their way back to their apartments on the floors above the 25th. The raiders had been hurled back. Torch-beams swerved across the walls in a lunatic semaphore. Laing slipped in a pool of grease and fell among the swerving shadows. Behind him, an excited woman stepped on his hand, her heel cutting his wrist.

For the next two hours a series of running battles took place in the corridors and staircases, moving up and down the floors as the barricades were reassembled and torn down again. At midnight, as he crouched in the elevator lobby behind the overturned fire-door, debating whether to risk making a run for Alice's apartment, Laing saw Richard Wilder standing among the scattered steel chairs. In one hand he still held his cine-camera. Like a large animal pausing for breath, he followed the huge projections of himself cast upon the walls and ceiling, as if about to leap on to the backs of his own shadows and ride them like a troupe of beasts up the flues of the building.

The confrontation subsided, moving away like a storm towards the lower floors. Laing and his neighbours assembled in Adrian Talbot's apartment. Here they sat on the living-room floor among the broken tables and the easy chairs with their slashed cushions. The torches at their feet formed a circle of light, shining on the bottles of whisky and vodka they shared together.

Arm in a sling, the psychiatrist moved around his vandalized apartment, trying to hang the shattered picture-frames over the slogans aerosolled across his walls in the supermarket paint-section's most fashionable colours. Talbot seemed more numbed by the personal hostility in these anti-homosexual obscenities than by the wholesale destruction of his apartment, but in spite of himself Laing found them stimulating. The lurid caricatures on the walls glimmered in the torch-light like the priapic figures drawn by cave-dwellers.

'At least they've left you alone,' Talbot said, crouching beside Laing. 'I've obviously been picked out as a scapegoat. This building must have been a powerhouse of resentments – everyone's working off the most extraordinary backlog of infantile aggressions.'

'They'll spend themselves.'

'Perhaps. I had a bucket of urine thrown over me this afternoon. Much more of that and I may take up a cudgel myself. It's a mistake to imagine that we're all moving towards a state of happy primitivism. The model here seems to be less the noble savage than our un-innocent post-Freudian selves, outraged by all that over-indulgent toilet-training, dedicated breast-feeding and parental affection – obviously a more dangerous mix than anything our Victorian forebears had to cope with. Our neighbours had happy childhoods to a man and still feel angry. Perhaps they resent never having had a chance to become perverse …'

As they nursed their bruises and passed around the bottles, drinking steadily to build up their courage, Laing listened to the talk of counter-attack and revenge. There was still no sign of Steele. For some reason Laing felt that he should have been there, a future leader more important to them than Crosland. In spite of his injuries, Laing felt exhilarated and confident, eager to return to the fray. The darkness was reassuring, providing its own security, the natural medium of their life in the apartment building. He felt proud of having learned how to move around the pitch-black corridors, never more than three steps at a time, how to pause and test the darkness, and even the right way of crossing his own apartment, always keeping as close to the floor as possible. He almost resented the daylight which the following morning would bring.

The true light of the high-rise was the metallic flash of the polaroid camera, that intermittent radiation which recorded a moment of hoped-for violence for some later voyeuristic pleasure. What depraved species of electric flora would spring to life from the garbage-strewn carpets of the corridors in response to this new source of light? The floors were littered with the blackened negative strips, flakes falling from this internal sun.

Muddled by alcohol and excitement, Laing clambered to his feet with his neighbours as they set off like a crowd of drunken students, brawling with each other to keep up their courage. By the time they had descended three floors in the darkness Laing had lost his bearings. They had entered an enclave of abandoned apartments on the 22nd floor. They wandered around the deserted rooms, kicking in the faces of the television sets, breaking up the kitchen crockery.

Trying to clear his head before going to rescue his sister, Laing vomited over a balcony rail. The threads of luminous phlegm fell away across the face of the building. Leaning there in the darkness, he listened to his neighbours moving along the corridor. When they had gone he would be able to look for Alice.

Behind him the electric lights came on. Startled, Laing flinched against the parapet, expecting an intruder to attack him. After a brief interval, the lights began to flicker continuously like a fibrillating heart. Laing looked down at his grimy clothes and vomit-stained hands. The vandalized living-room glimmered around him, the floor strewn with debris as if he had woken on a battlefield.

In the bedroom a broken mirror lay on the bed, the pieces flickering like the fragments of another world trying unsuccessfully to reconstitute itself.

'Come in, Laing ...' The familiar precise voice of the orthodontic surgeon called out to him. 'There's something interesting here.'

Steele was circling the room with a sword-stick in one hand. Now and then he feinted at the floor in a teasing way, as if rehearsing a scene from a melodrama. He beckoned Laing forward into the stuttering light.

Laing cautiously approached the door, glad to see Steele at last but well aware of how exposed he was to any passing whim of his. He assumed that Steele had trapped the apartment's owner, or a vagrant resident who had taken shelter here, but there was no one in the room. Then, following the blade of the sword-stick, he saw that Steele had cornered a small cat between the legs of the dressing-table. Steele lunged forward, twirling a brocade curtain he had wrenched from the window, and whirled the terrified creature into the bathroom.

'Wait, doctor!' The surgeon's voice was infused with a strangely cold gaiety, like an erotic machine's. 'Don't leave yet ...'

The lights continued to flicker with the harsh over-reality of an atrocity newsreel. Confused by his own response, Laing watched Steele manipulate the cat under the curtain. By some ugly logic the dentist's pleasure in tormenting the creature was doubled by the presence of a squeamish but fascinated witness. Laing stood in the bathroom doorway, hoping despite himself that the lights would not fail again. He waited as Steele calmly smothered the cat, destroying it under the curtain as if carrying out a complex resuscitation under a hospital blanket.

Pulling himself away at last, Laing left without speaking. He moved carefully along the darkened corridor, as the lights flickered from the doorways of ransacked apartments, from overturned lamps lying on the floor and television screens brought back to a last intermittent life. A faint music played somewhere around him. An abandoned record turntable was spinning again. In an empty bedroom a cine-projector screened the last feet of a pornographic film on to the wall facing the bed.

When he reached Alice's apartment Laing hesitated, uncertain how to explain his presence. But as his sister opened the door and beckoned him in he saw immediately that she had known he was coming. Two suitcases, already packed, stood in the living-room. Alice walked to the door of her bedroom for the last time. In the yellow, intermittent light Frobisher was slumped asleep on the bed, a half-empty case of whisky beside him.

Alice took Laing's arm. 'You're late,' she said reprovingly. 'I've been waiting for hours.' As they left she made no attempt to look back at her husband. Laing remembered Alice and himself at home years earlier, and how once they had slipped out of the drawing-room in the same way as their mother lay unconscious on the floor after injuring herself during a drinking bout.

The sounds of a minor clash echoed up the stairwell as they made their way to the safety of the darkness on the 25th floor. Fifteen floors, including Laing's own, were now permanently without light.

Like a storm reluctant to end, recapitulating itself at intervals, the violence rumbled on throughout the night as Laing and his sister lay awake together on the mattress in his bedroom.

12

TOWARDS THE SUMMIT

Soon after two o'clock in the afternoon four days later, Richard Wilder returned from his television station and drove into the parking-lot beside the high-rise. Reducing speed so that he could relish to the full this moment of arrival, he sat back comfortably behind the wheel and looked up with a confident eye at the face of the apartment building. Around him the long ranks of parked cars were covered with a thickening layer of dirt and cement dust, blown across the open plazas of the development project from the road junction under construction behind the medical centre. Few cars now left the parking-lot, and there were almost no free spaces, but Wilder drove up and down the access lanes, stopping at the end of each file and reversing back to his starting point.

Wilder fingered the freshly healed scar on his unshaven chin, relic of a vigorous corridor battle the previous night. Deliberately he reopened the wound and glanced with satisfaction at the point of blood on his finger. He had driven from the television station at speed, as if trying to emerge from an angry dream, shouting and sounding the horn at other drivers in his way, cutting up one-way streets. Now he felt calm and relaxed. The first sight of the line of five apartment buildings soothed him as usual, providing a context of reality absent from the studios.

Confident that he would find a free space, Wilder continued his patrol. Originally he had parked, along with his neighbours on the lower floors, in the ranks along the perimeter of the parking-lot, but during the previous weeks he had been moving his car nearer to the building. What had begun as a harmless piece of vanity – an ironic joke at his own expense – had soon taken on a more serious role, a visible index of his success or failure. After several weeks dedicated to his ascent of the building he felt entitled to park in those files reserved for his new neighbours. Ultimately he would reach the front rank. At the moment of his triumph, when he climbed to the 40th floor, his car would join the line of expensive wrecks nearest to the apartment block.

For several hours the previous night Wilder had reached the 20th floor and even, during the few minutes of an unexpected skirmish, the 25th. By dawn he had been forced to retire from this advance position to his present base camp, an apartment on the 17th floor owned by a stage manager at the television station, a former drinking companion named Hillman who had grudgingly accepted this cuckoo in his nest. The occupation of a floor, in Wilder's strict sense of the term, meant more than the casual seizure of an abandoned apartment. Dozens of these were scattered throughout the high-rise. Wilder had imposed on himself a harder definition of ascent – he had to be accepted by his new neighbours as one of them, the holder of a tenancy won by something other than physical force. In short, he insisted that they need him – when he thought about it, a notion that made him snort.

He had reached the 20th floor as a result of one of the many demographic freaks that had confused his progress through the building. During the running battles that had filled the night he found himself helping to barricade the damaged door of an apartment on the 20th floor owned by two women stock-market analysts. After trying to brain him with a champagne bottle as he pushed his head through the broken panel, they had welcomed Wilder's easy-going offer to help – he deliberately was never more calm than at these moments of crisis. In fact, the older of the two, a spirited blonde of thirty, had complimented Wilder on being the only sane man she had met in the high-rise. For his part, Wilder was glad to play a domestic role rather than the populist leader and Bonaparte of the elevator-lobby barricades, instructing an ill-trained militia of magazine editors and finance company executives in how to storm a defended staircase or capture a rival elevator. Apart from anything else, the higher up the building he climbed, the worse the physical condition of the residents – hours on the gymnasium exercycles had equipped them for no more than hours on the gymnasium exercycles.

After helping the two women, he spent the period before dawn drinking their wine and manoeuvring them into making the suggestion that he move into their apartment. As usual, he gestured grandly with his cine-camera and told them about his television documentary on the high-rise, inviting them to appear on screen. But neither was particularly impressed by the offer. Although the lower-level tenants were keen to take part in the programme and vent their grievances, the people living on the upper floors had appeared on television already, often more than once, as professional experts on various current-affairs programmes. 'Television is for watching, Wilder,' one of the women told him firmly, 'not for appearing on.'

Soon after dawn, the members of a women's raiding-party appeared. Their husbands and companions had either moved in with friends on other floors or exited from their lives altogether. The leader of the pack, the elderly children's-story writer, gazed balefully at Wilder when he offered her the starring role in his documentary. Taking the hint, Wilder bowed out and returned to his previously secure base, the Hillmans' apartment on the 17th floor.

Thirty feet away, as Wilder drove around the parking-lot, determined to find a rank in keeping with his new station, a bottle shattered across a car roof, vanishing in a brittle cloud-burst. The bottle had been dropped from a height, conceivably from the 40th floor. Wilder slowed his car almost to a halt, offering himself as a target. He half-expected to see the white-jacketed figure of Anthony Royal standing in one of his messianic poses on the parapet of his penthouse, the white Alsatian at his heels.

During the past days he had caught several glimpses of the architect, standing high above Wilder at the top of a staircase, disappearing in a commandeered elevator towards the fastnesses of the top floors. Without any doubt, he was deliberately exposing himself to Wilder, tempting him upwards. At times Royal seemed to be uncannily aware of the confused image of his natural father that hovered in the attics of Wilder's mind, glimpsed always in the high windows of his nursery. Had Royal set out to play this role, knowing that Wilder's confusions about his father would deflect his resolve to climb the building? Wilder drummed his heavy fists on the steering wheel. Each night he moved closer to Royal, a few steps nearer their ultimate confrontation.

Broken glass crackled under his tyres, as if unzipping the treads. Directly ahead of Wilder, in the front rank reserved for the top-floor residents, was a free space once occupied by the dead jeweller's car. Without hesitating, Wilder spun the wheel and steered into the open space.

'Not before time ...'

He sat back expansively, gazing with pleasure at the garbage-strewn wrecks on either side. The appearance of the space was a good omen. He took his time getting out of the car, and slammed the door aggressively. As he strode towards the entrance he felt like a well-to-do landowner who had just bought himself a mountain.

In the entrance lobby a group of down-at-heel 1st-floor residents watched Wilder stride past the elevators to the stairway. They were suspicious of his movements around the building, his changing allegiances. During the day Wilder spent a few hours with Helen and his sons in the 2nd-floor apartment, trying to rally his increasingly withdrawn wife. Sooner or later he would have to leave her for ever. In the evenings, when he renewed his ascent of the high-rise, she would come alive a little, perhaps even speak to him about his work at the television studios, referring to programmes on which he had worked years before. The previous night, as he prepared to leave, settling his sons and testing the locks on the doors, Helen had suddenly embraced him, as if wanting him to stay. The muscles of her thin face had moved through an irregular sequence of tremors, like tumblers trying to fall into place.

To Wilder's surprise, when he returned to the apartment he found Helen in a state of high excitement. He made his way around the garbage-sacks and barricades of broken furniture that blocked the corridor. Helen and a group of wives were celebrating a minor triumph. The tired women with their unruly children – the civil war within the high-rise had made them as combative as their parents – formed a wistful tenement tableau.

Two young women from the 7th floor, who had once worked as teachers in the junior school, had volunteered to reopen the classes. From their uneasy glances at the vigilante group of three fathers – a computer-time salesman, a sound man and a travel-agency courier – standing between them and the door Wilder guessed that they were the victims of a less than gentle abduction.

As he prepared a meal from the last of the canned food, Helen sat at the kitchen table, her white hands moving about like a pair of confused birds in a cage.

'I can barely believe it – I'll be free of the boys for an hour or two.'

'Where are these classes being held?'

'Here – for the next two mornings. It's the least I can do.'

'But you won't be away from the boys at all. Well, anything's better than nothing.'

Would she ever abandon the children? Wilder asked himself. It was all she thought about. As he played with his sons he seriously considered taking them with him on his climb. He watched Helen making a nervous effort to tidy the apartment. The living-room had been ransacked during a raid. While Helen and the boys sheltered in a neighbour's apartment, most of the furniture had been broken, the kitchen kicked to a shambles. Helen carried the wrecked chairs from the dining-room, lining them up in front of Wilder's broken-backed desk. The tilting chairs leaned against each other in a scarecrow parody of a children's classroom.

Wilder made no effort to help. He watched her thin arms dragging at the furniture. At times he almost suspected that she was deliberately exhausting herself, and that the bruises on her wrists and knees were part of an elaborate system of conscious self-mutilation, an attempt to win back her husband – each day when he returned home he half expected to find her in an invalid chair, legs broken and trepan bandage around her shaven head, about to take the last desperate step of lobotomy.

Why did he keep coming back to her? His one ambition now was to get away from Helen, and overcome that need to return to the apartment each afternoon and whatever threadbare links it maintained with his own childhood. By leaving Helen he would break away from the whole system of juvenile restraints he had been trying to shake off since his adolescence. Even his compulsive womanizing was part of the same attempt to free himself from the past, an attempt that Helen brought to nothing by turning a blind eye. At least, however, his affairs had prepared the ground for his ascent of the high-rise, those literal handholds which would carry him on his climb to the roof over the supine bodies of the women he had known.

He found it difficult now to feel much involvement with his wife's plight, or with her neighbours and their narrow, defeated lives. Already it was clear that the lower floors were doomed. Even their insistence on educating their children, the last reflex of any exploited group before it sank into submission, marked the end of their resistance. Helen was even being helped now by the women's group from the 29th floor. During the noon armistice the children's-story writer and her minions moved through the apartment building, offering help to abandoned or isolated wives, sisters of sinister charity.

Wilder went into his sons' bedroom. Glad to see Wilder, they banged their empty feeding-bowls with their plastic machine-pistols. They were dressed in miniature paratroopers' camouflage suits and tin helmets – the wrong outfit, Wilder reflected, in the light of what had been taking place in the high-rise. The correct combat costume was stockbroker's pin-stripe, briefcase and homburg.

The boys were hungry. After calling to Helen he returned to the kitchen. Helen was slumped on her knees in front of the electric cooker. The door was open, and Wilder had the sudden notion that she was trying to hide her small body in the oven – perhaps cook herself, the ultimate sacrifice for her family.

'Helen ...' He bent down, surprised by the slightness of her body, a collection of sticks inside her pallid skin. For heaven's sake, you're like ...'

'It's all right ... I'll have something later.' She pulled herself away from him, and began to pick without thinking at the burnt fat on the oven floor. Looking down at her huddled at his feet, Wilder realized that she had momentarily fainted from hunger.

Wilder let her subside against the cooker. He scanned the empty shelves of the pantry. 'Stay here – I'll go up to the supermarket and get you something to eat.' Angry with her, he snapped, 'Why didn't you tell me you were starving yourself?'

'Richard, I've mentioned it a hundred times.'

She watched him from the floor as he hunted in her purse for money, something Wilder had found less and less use for recently. He had not even bothered to pay his latest salary cheque into his account. He picked up his cine-camera, making sure that the lens shroud was in place. As he looked back at Helen he noticed that her eyes were surprisingly hard within her small face, almost as if she was amused by her husband's dependence on the fictions of this elaborate toy.

Locking the apartment door behind him, Wilder set off in search of food and water. During the afternoon lull, one access route to the 10th-floor supermarket was still allowed the tenants in the lower section of the apartment building. Most of the stairways were blocked by permanent barricades – living-room furniture, dining-tables and washing-machines piled high between the steps and ceilings. More than a dozen of the twenty elevators were out of order. The remainder functioned intermittently, at the whim of any superior clan.

In the lobby Wilder peered cautiously up the empty shafts. Sections of metal railing and water pipes criss-crossed the shafts, inserted like stop indicators to prevent the cars moving up or down, and almost formed a staircase of their own.

The walls were covered with slogans and obscenities, lists of apartments to be vandalized like an insane directory. By the stairwell doors a military-style message in sober lettering pointed to the one safe staircase to be used during the early afternoon, and the obligatory curfew time, three o'clock.

Wilder raised his camera and stared at the message through the view-finder. The shot would make a striking opening title sequence for the documentary on the high-rise. He was still aware of the need to make a visual record of what had happened within the apartment building, but the resolve had begun to fade. The decline of the apartment building reminded him of a slow-motion newsreel of a town in the Andes being carried down the mountain slopes to its death, the inhabitants still hanging out their washing in the disintegrating gardens, cooking in their kitchens as the walls were pulverized around them.

Twenty of the floors in the high-rise were now in darkness at night, and over a hundred apartments had been abandoned by their owners. The clan system, which had once given a measure of security to the residents, had now largely broken down, individual groups drifting into apathy or paranoia. Everywhere people were retreating into their apartments, even into one room, and barricading themselves away. At the 5th-floor landing Wilder paused, surprised that there was no one around. He waited by the lobby doors, listening for any suspicious sound. The tall figure of a middle-aged sociologist, garbage-pail in hand, emerged from the shadows and drifted like a ghost along the refuse-strewn corridor.

For all the building's derelict state – almost no water was flowing, the air-conditioning vents were blocked with garbage and excrement, rails ripped off the staircase balustrades – the behaviour of the residents during the daylight hours for the most part remained restrained. At the 7th-floor landing Wilder stopped and relieved himself against the steps. In a way he was surprised by the sight of the urine running away between his feet. However, this was the mildest display of crudity. During the brawls and running battles of the night he was aware that he took a distinct and unguilty pleasure in urinating wherever he cared, defecating in abandoned apartments regardless of the health hazards to himself and his family. The previous night he had enjoyed pushing around a terrified woman who remonstrated with him for relieving himself on her bathroom floor.

None the less, Wilder welcomed and understood the night – only in the darkness could one become sufficiently obsessive, deliberately play on all one's repressed instincts. He welcomed this forced conscription of the deviant strains in his character. Happily, this free and degenerate behaviour became easier the higher he moved up the building, as if encouraged by the secret logic of the high-rise.

The 10th-floor concourse was deserted. Wilder pushed back the staircase doors with their shattered glass and walked out on to the shopping mall. The bank had closed, along with the hairdressing salon and the liquor store. The last supermarket cashier – the wife of a cameraman on the 3rd floor – sat stoically at her check-out point, presiding like a doomed Britannia over a sea of debris. Wilder strolled around the empty shelves. Rotting packs floated in the greasy water at the bottom of the freezer cabinets. In the centre of the supermarket a pyramid of dog-biscuit cartons had collapsed across the aisle.

Wilder filled a basket with three of the cartons and half a dozen cans of cat-meat. Together they would keep Helen and the boys alive until he could break into an apartment and raid a food cache.

'There's nothing here but pet food,' he told the cashier at the check-out. 'Have you stopped ordering?'

'There's no demand,' she told him. She played absent-mindedly with an open wound on her forehead. 'Everyone must have stocked up months ago.'

This was not true, Wilder reflected as he walked away towards the elevator lobby, leaving her alone on the huge concourse. As he knew full well, having broken into any number of apartments, few people had any reserve supplies whatever. It was as if they were no longer giving any thought to what they might need the next day.

Fifty feet away, beyond the overturned hair-driers lying outside the salon, the elevator indicator lights moved from right to left. The last public elevator of the day was winding itself up the building. Somewhere between the 25th and 30th floors it would be brought to a halt at the whim of a lookout, marking the end of the mid-day armistice and the beginnings of another night.

Without thinking, Wilder quickened his pace. He reached the doors as the elevator paused at the 9th floor to discharge a passenger. At the last moment, as it resumed its ascent, Wilder pressed the button.

In the few seconds that remained before the doors opened he realized that he had already decided to abandon Helen and his sons for good. Only one direction lay before him – up. Like a climber resting a hundred feet from the summit, he had no option but to ascend.

The elevator doors opened. Some fifteen passengers faced him, standing rigidly together like plastic mannequins. There was a fractional movement of feet as a space was made for Wilder.

Wilder hesitated, controlling his impulse to turn and run down the staircase to his apartment. The eyes of the passengers were fixed on him, wary of his indecision and suspecting that it might conceal a ruse of some kind.

As the doors began to close Wilder stepped forward into the elevator, the cine-camera raised in front of him, and began once again his ascent of the high-rise.

13

BODY MARKINGS

After a delay of twenty minutes, as irritating as a hold-up at a provincial frontier post, the elevator moved from the 16th to the 17th floor. Exhausted by the long wait, Wilder stepped through the doors into the lobby, looking for somewhere to throw away his cartons of pet food. Crammed together shoulder to shoulder, the returning cost-accountants and television executives held tightly to their briefcases, eyes averted from each other as they stared at the graffiti on the walls of the car. The steel roof had been removed, and the long shaft rose above their heads, exposed to anyone with a missile casually to hand.

The three passengers who stepped out with Wilder vanished among the barricades that lined the dimly lit corridors. When Wilder reached the Hillmans' apartment he found that the door was securely bolted. There were no sounds of movement from within. Wilder tried without success to force the lock. Conceivably the Hillmans had abandoned the apartment and taken shelter with friends. Then he heard a faint scraping from the hall. Pressing his head to the door, he heard Mrs Hillman remonstrating with herself in a thin voice as she pulled a heavy object across the floor.

After a prolonged tapping and negotiation, during which Wilder was obliged to speak to her in her own wheedling tone, he was admitted to the apartment. A huge barricade of furniture, units of kitchen equipment, books, clothes and table ornaments blocked the hallway, a miniature municipal dump in its own right.

Hillman lay on a mattress in the bedroom. His head was bandaged in a torn evening-dress shirt, through which the blood had seeped on to the pillow. He raised his head as Wilder came in, his hand searching for a section of balcony railing on the floor beside him. Hillman had been one of the first scapegoats to be selected and attacked – his brusque and independent manner made him a natural target. During a raid on the next floor he had been hit on the head by a television award-winner's statuette as he tried to order his way up a defended staircase. Wilder had carried him back to his apartment and spent the night looking after him.

With her husband out of commission, Mrs Hillman depended totally on Wilder, a dependence that he himself in a way enjoyed. When Wilder was away she spent all her time worrying about him, like an over-anxious mother fretting about a wayward child, though as soon as he arrived she forgot who he was.

She tugged at Wilder's sleeve as he looked down at Hillman. She was more concerned about her barricade than her husband and his ominous disturbances of vision. Almost everything movable in the apartment, however small, she had added to the barricade, at times threatening to entomb them for good. Each night Wilder slept through the few hours before dawn slumped in an armchair partly embedded in the barricade. He would hear her moving tirelessly around him, adding a small piece of furniture she had found somewhere, three books, a single gramophone record, her jewellery box. Once Wilder woke to find that she had incorporated part of his left leg. Often it would take him half an hour to dig his way out of the apartment.

'What is it?' Wilder asked her irritably. 'What are you doing to my arm?' She was peering at the bag of dog-food, which Wilder, in the absence of any furniture, had been unable to put down. For some reason, he did not want it added to the barricade.

'I've been cleaning up for you,' she told him with some pride. 'You wanted me to, didn't you?'

'Of course ...' Wilder gazed around the apartment in a lordly way. In fact, he barely noticed any changes and, if anything, preferred the apartment to be dirty.

'What's this?' She poked excitedly at the carton, jabbing him roguishly in the ribs as if she had caught a small son with a secret present for her. 'You've got a surprise!'

'Leave it alone.' Roughly, Wilder fended her away, almost knocking her off her feet. In a way, he enjoyed these absurd rituals. They touched levels of intimacy that had never been possible with Helen. The higher up the building he moved the more free he felt to play these games.

Mrs Hillman wrestled a pack of dog-biscuits out of the bag. Her small body was surprisingly agile. She gazed at the overweight basset hound on the label. Both she and her husband were as thin as scarecrows. Generously, Wilder handed her a can of cat-meat.

'Soak the biscuits in gin – I know you've got a bottle hidden somewhere. It will do you both good.'

'We'll get a dog!' When Wilder looked irritated by this suggestion she sidled up to him teasingly, pressing her hands against his heavy chest. 'A dog? Please, Dicky ...'

Wilder tried to move away from her, but the lewd, wheedling tone and the pressure of her fingers on his nipples unsettled him. Their unexpected sexual expertise excited a hidden strain in his character. Hillman, the dress shirt around his head like a bloody turban, was looking up passively at them, his face drained of all colour. With his visual disturbances, Wilder reflected, the empty apartment would seem to be filled with embracing replicas of himself and Mrs Hillman. He pretended to accost her, out of curiosity running his hands over her buttocks, as small as apples, to see how the injured man would react. But Hillman gave no flicker of recognition.

Wilder stopped stroking Mrs Hillman when he saw that she was openly responding to him. It was on other levels that he wanted their relationship to develop.

'Dicky, I know why you came to rescue me ...' Mrs Hillman followed him around the barricade, still holding Wilder's arm. 'Will you punish them?'

This was another of their games. 'Rescue' she visualized primarily in terms of making 'them' – that is, all the residents in the high-rise below the 17th floor – eat humble pie and prostrate themselves in an endless line outside her front door.

'I'll punish them,' Wilder reassured her. 'All right?'

They were leaning against the barricade, Mrs Hillman's sharp-chinned face against his chest. No more ill-suited couple, Wilder decided, could have been cast to play mock-mother and mock-son. Nodding eagerly at the prospect of revenge, Mrs Hillman reached into the barricade and pulled at a black metal pipe. As it emerged, Wilder saw that it was the barrel of a shotgun.

Surprised, Wilder took the weapon from her hands. She was smiling encouragingly, as if expecting Wilder to go out into the corridor at that very moment and shoot someone dead. He broke the breech. Two live shells were in place under the hammers.

Wilder moved the weapon out of Mrs Hillman's reach. He realized that this was probably only one of hundreds of similar firearms in the high-rise – sporting rifles, military service souvenirs, handbag pistols. But no one had fired a single shot, despite the epidemic of violence. Wilder knew perfectly well why. He himself would never bring himself to fire this shotgun, even at the point of death. There was an unspoken agreement among the residents of the high-rise that their confrontation would be resolved by physical means alone.

He jammed the shotgun back into the barricade and pushed Mrs Hillman in the chest. 'Go away, rescue yourself …'

As she protested, half-playfully, half in earnest, he began to throw dog-biscuits at her, scattering them around the bare floor. Wilder enjoyed abusing her. Deriding her in front of her supine husband, he withheld the food from her until she broke down and retreated to the kitchen. The evening progressed happily. Wilder became more and more oafish as the darkness settled over the high-rise, deliberately coarsening himself like a delinquent youth fooling about with a besotted headmistress.

Until two o'clock that morning, during a night intermittently disrupted by outbreaks of violence, Wilder remained within the Hillmans' apartment on the 17th floor. The marked decline in the number of incidents disturbed Wilder – for his ascent of the building he relied on being able to offer himself as an aggressive street-fighter to one or another of the warring groups. However, the open tribal conflicts of the previous week had now clearly ceased. With the breakdown of the clan structure, the formal boundary and armistice lines had dissolved, giving way to a series of small enclaves, a cluster of three or four isolated apartments. These were far more difficult to penetrate and exploit.

Sitting in the darkness on the floor of the sitting-room with Mrs Hillman, their backs to opposite walls, they listened to the muted noises around them. The residents of the high-rise were like creatures in a darkened zoo lying together in surly quiet, now and then tearing at each other in brief acts of ferocious violence.

The Hillmans' immediate neighbours, an insurance broker and his wife, two account executives and a pharmacologist, were listless and unorganized. Wilder had visited them several times, but found that appeals to self-advantage no longer roused them. In fact, only the most blatant expressions of irrational hostility could galvanize their glazed minds. Wilder's feigned and unfeigned rages, his fantasies of revenge roused them briefly from their state of torpor.

This regrouping around more radical and aggressive leaders was taking place all over the high-rise. In the hours after midnight torches flared behind the barricades in the lobbies and corridors, where enclaves of five or six residents squatted among the plastic garbage-sacks, inciting each other like wedding guests making themselves drunk in the knowledge that they too will soon be copulating freely among the sweetmeats.

At two o'clock Wilder left the Hillmans' apartment and set about stirring up his neighbours. The men crouched together, clubs and spears in hand, hip-flasks of whisky pooled at their feet. The torch-beams illuminated the garbage-sacks piled high around them, a visible museum of their leavings. Wilder sat in the centre of the group, outlining his plans for another foraging expedition to the floors above. Although they had eaten little for days, his neighbours were reluctant to take part, fearful of the power of the residents above them. Skilfully, Wilder played on their fantasies. Once again, as his imaginary scapegoat, he selected the psychiatrist Adrian Talbot, whom he now accused of molesting a child in a swimming-pool changing cubicle. The untruth of the accusation, which they all well knew, only served to reinforce it. However, before they would move they insisted that Wilder invent an even more lurid crime, as if the imaginary nature of Talbot's sexual offences held the essence of their appeal. By the logic of the high-rise those most innocent of any offence became the most guilty.

Shortly before dawn Wilder found himself in an empty apartment on the 26th floor. Once occupied by a woman and her small son, the apartment had recently been abandoned, and no attempt had been made to padlock the door from the outside. Tired after the night's rampage, Wilder wasted no time in breaking down the door. He had side-stepped his raiding party, leaving them to break up Talbot's apartment for the tenth time. During these last minutes of darkness he would settle himself into an empty apartment, and sleep through the long hours of daylight in time to resume his ascent of the high-rise at dusk.

Wilder moved around the three rooms, satisfying himself that no one was hiding in the kitchen or bathroom. He wandered about in the darkness, kicking open the cupboards and knocking any books or ornaments to the floor. Before leaving, the owner had made a half-hearted attempt to tidy the apartment, packing away the child's toys in a bedroom wardrobe. The sight of the freshly swept floors and neatly furled curtains unsettled Wilder. He pulled the drawers on to the floor, heaved the mattresses off the beds, and urinated into the bath. His burly figure, trousers open to expose his heavy genitalia, glared at him from the mirrors in the bedroom. He was about to break the glass, but the sight of his penis calmed him, a white club hanging in the darkness. He would have liked to dress it in some way, perhaps with a hair-ribbon tied in a floral bow.

Now that he was alone Wilder felt confident of his progress. His hunger was overlaid by his feelings of triumph at having climbed more than half-way up the high-rise. From the windows the ground below was barely visible, part of a world he had left behind. Somewhere above him, Anthony Royal was strutting about with his white Alsatian, unaware that he would soon be in for a surprise.

At dawn the owner of the apartment reappeared, and blundered into the kitchen where Wilder was resting. By now he had relaxed and was sitting comfortably on the floor with his back against the cooker, the remains of a meal scattered around him.

He had found the few cans of food, along with two bottles of red wine, in their invariable hiding place, under the floorboards in the bedroom wardrobe. As he broke open the cans he played with a battery-powered tape-recorder which had been mixed up with the child's toys. He recorded his grunts and belches, playing them back to himself. Wilder was amused by the deft way in which he edited the tape, overlaying one set of belches with a second and third, a skill that now resided entirely in his scarred fingers with their cracked and blackened nails.

The bottles of claret had made him pleasantly drowsy. Smearing the red wine across his broad chest, he gazed up amiably at the startled woman who stumbled into the kitchen and tripped across his legs.

As she stared down at him, one hand nervously to her throat, Wilder remembered that she had once been called Charlotte Melville. The name had now detached itself from her, like an athlete's tie-on numeral blown away in a gust of wind. He knew that he had often been in this apartment, and this explained the vague familiarity of the child's toys and the furniture, although the chairs and sofa had been rearranged to conceal various hiding places.

'Wilder ...?' As if uncertain about the name, Charlotte Melville pronounced it softly. She had been sheltering during the night with her son in the apartment of the statistician three floors above with whom she had become friendly. At the first light, when everything had settled down, she had come back intending to collect the last of her food reserves before abandoning the apartment for good. Swiftly composing herself, she looked down critically at the burly man with the exposed loins lying like a savage among her wine bottles, his chest painted with red stripes. She felt no sense of loss or outrage, but a fatalistic acceptance of the damage he had casually inflicted on her apartment, like the strong odour of his urine in the bathroom.

He appeared to be half asleep, and she stepped slowly towards the door. Wilder reached out with one hand and held her ankle. He smiled up at her blearily. Climbing to his feet, he circled around her, the tape-recorder raised in one hand as if about to hit her with it. Instead he switched it on and off, playing for her his selection of belches and grunts, obviously pleased with this demonstration of his unexpected expertise. He steered her slowly around the apartment as she backed from one room to the next, listening to his edited mutterings.

The first time he struck her, cuffing her to the bedroom floor, he tried to record her gasp, but the reel had jammed. He freed it carefully, bent down and slapped her again, only stopping when he had recorded her now deliberate cries to his satisfaction. He enjoyed terrorizing her, taping down her exaggerated but none the less frightened gasps. During their clumsy sexual act on the mattress in the child's bedroom he left the tape-recorder switched on beside them on the floor and played back the sounds of this brief rape, editing together the noise of her tearing clothes and panting anger.

Later, bored with the woman and these games with the tape-recorder, he hurled the machine into the corner. The sound of himself speaking, however coarsely, introduced a discordant element. He resented speaking to Charlotte or to anyone else, as if words introduced the wrong set of meanings into everything.

After she dressed they had breakfast together on the balcony, sitting at the table with an incongruous old-world formality. Charlotte ate the scraps of canned meat she found on the kitchen floor. Wilder finished the last of the claret, remarking the red stripes across his chest. The rising sunlight warmed his exposed loins, and he felt like a contented husband sitting with his wife in a villa high on a mountainside. Naively, he wanted to explain to Charlotte his ascent of the apartment building, and shyly pointed to the roof. But she failed to get the point. She fastened her torn clothes around her strong body. Although her mouth and throat were bruised, she seemed unconcerned, watching Wilder with a passive expression.

From the balcony Wilder could see the roof of the high-rise, little more than a dozen floors above him. The intoxication of living at this height was as palpable as anything produced by the wine bottle in his hand. Already he could see the line of huge birds perched on the balustrades, no doubt waiting for him to arrive and take command.

Below, on the 20th floor, a man was cooking over a fire on his balcony, breaking up a coffee table and feeding the legs to the clutch of smouldering sticks on which a soup can was balanced.

A police car approached the perimeter entrance. A few residents were leaving for work at this early hour, neatly dressed in suits and raincoats, briefcases in hand. The abandoned cars in the access roads prevented the police from reaching the main entrance to the building, and the officers stepped out and spoke to the passing residents. Usually none of them would have replied to an outsider, but now they gathered in a group around the two policemen. Wilder wondered if they were going to give the game away, but although he could not hear them, he was certain that he knew what they were saying. Clearly they were pacifying the policemen, reassuring them that everything was in order, despite the garbage and broken bottles scattered around the building.

Deciding to test the defences of the apartment before he went to sleep, Wilder stepped into the corridor. He stood outside the doorway, as the stale air moved past him to the open balcony. He relished the rich smells of the high-rise. Like their garbage, the excrement of the residents higher up the building had a markedly different odour.

Returning to the balcony, he watched the police drive away in their car. Of the twenty or so residents who still left for work each morning, three had turned back, evidently unsettled by the task of convincing the police that all was well. Without looking up, they scurried back to the entrance lobby.

Wilder knew that they would never leave again. The separation of the high-rise from the world around it was now almost complete, and would probably coincide with his own arrival at the summit. Soothed by this image, he sat down on the floor and leaned against Charlotte Melville's shoulder, falling asleep as she stroked the wine-coloured stripes on his chest and shoulders.

14

FINAL TRIUMPH

At dusk, after he had strengthened the guard, Anthony Royal ordered the candles lit on the dining-room table. Hands in the pockets of his dinner-jacket, he stood at the windows of the penthouse apartment on the 40th floor and looked down across the concrete plazas of the development project. All the tenants who had earlier left for their offices had now parked their cars and entered the building. With their safe arrival, Royal felt for the first time that he could relax, like a captain eager to set sail seeing the last of his crew return from shore-leave in a foreign port. The evening had begun.

Royal sat down in the high-backed oak chair at the head of the dining-table. The candlelight flickered over the silver cutlery and gold plate, reflected in the silk facings of his dinner-jacket. As usual he smiled at the theatricality of this contrived setting, like a badly rehearsed and under-financed television commercial for a high-life product. It had started three weeks earlier when he and Pangbourne had decided to dress for dinner each evening. Royal had ordered the women to extend the dining-room table to its furthest length, so that he could sit with his back to the high windows and the illuminated decks of the nearby buildings. Responding to Royal, the women had brought candles and silverware from secret caches, and served an elaborately prepared meal. Their shadows swayed across the ceiling as if they were moving around the dining chamber of a feudal chief. Sitting in his chair at the far end of the long table, Pangbourne had been suitably impressed.

Of course, as the gynaecologist well knew, the charade was meaningless. A single step beyond the circle of candle-light the garbage-sacks were piled six-deep against the walls. Outside, the corridors and staircases were filled with broken furniture and barricades built from washing-machines and freezer cabinets. The elevator shafts were the new garbage chutes. Not one of the twenty elevators in the apartment building now functioned, and the shafts were piled deep with kitchen refuse and dead dogs. A fading semblance of civilized order still survived in the top three floors, the last tribal unit in the high-rise. However, the one error that Royal and Pangbourne had made was to assume that there would always be some kind of social organization below them which they could exploit and master. They were now moving into a realm of no social organization at all. The clans had broken down into small groups of killers, solitary hunters who built man-traps in empty apartments or preyed on the unwary in deserted elevator lobbies.

Royal looked up from the polished table as one of the women walked into the room, a silver tray in her strong arms. Watching her, he remembered that she was Mrs Wilder. She wore one of Anne's well-cut trouser-suits, and not for the first time Royal thought how easily this intelligent woman had fitted into the upper levels of the high-rise. Two weeks earlier, when she was found cowering with her sons in an empty apartment on the 19th floor after Wilder had abandoned her, she was totally exhausted, numbed by hunger and indignation. Whether in quest of her husband, or responding to some dim instinct, she had begun to climb the building. The raiding party brought her to the top floor. Pangbourne had wanted to throw out this anaemic and rambling woman, but Royal overruled him. Somewhere below, Wilder was still making his ascent of the high-rise, and his wife might one day be a valuable hostage. Led away, she joined the group of outcast wives who lived with their children in the next apartment, earning their keep by working as house servants.

Within days Mrs Wilder had regained her strength and self-confidence. No longer stunned and stoop-shouldered, she reminded Royal of the serious and attractive wife of an up-and-coming television journalist who had arrived at the high-rise a year earlier.

He noticed that she was clearing away Pangbourne's place setting, returning the immaculate silverware to her tray.

'They seem clean enough,' Royal told her. 'I don't think Dr Pangbourne will notice.' When she ignored him and continued to remove the cutlery. Royal asked, 'Have you heard from him? I take it he won't be joining me this evening?'

'Or any evening. He's decided to decline in future.' Mrs Wilder glanced across the table at Royal, almost as if she had felt a flicker of concern for him. She added matter-of-factly, 'I should be wary of Dr Pangbourne.'

'I always have been.'

'When a man like Dr Pangbourne loses his appetite for food it's reasonable to assume that he has something much more interesting between his teeth – and much more dangerous.'

Royal listened to her cool advice without comment. He was not surprised that the dinners had come to an end. Both he and Pangbourne, anticipating the inevitable break-up of the last clan within the apartment building, had now retired to their quarters at opposite ends of the roof, each taking his women with him. Pangbourne had moved into the penthouse once owned by the dead jeweller. Strangely enough, Royal reflected, they would soon be back where they had begun, each tenant isolated within his own apartment.

Something warned him to dispense with this meal but he waited for Mrs Wilder to serve him. Having survived so far, nothing that the gynaecologist could do would put him off his stride. During the past months almost all traces of his accident had vanished, and Royal felt stronger and more confident than ever before. He had won his attempt to dominate the high-rise, and amply proved his right to rule this huge building, even though at the cost of his marriage. As for the new social order that he had hoped to see emerge, he knew now that his original vision of a high-rise aviary had been closer to the truth than he guessed. Without knowing it, he had constructed a gigantic vertical zoo, its hundreds of cages stacked above each other. All the events of the past few months made sense if one realized that these brilliant and exotic creatures had learned to open the doors.

Royal sat back as Mrs Wilder served him. Since his own kitchen lacked any equipment, all his meals were prepared in the apartment next door. Mrs Wilder reappeared with her tray, stepping over the garbage-sacks that lined the hallway – for all their descent into barbarism, the residents of the high-rise remained faithful to their origins and continued to generate a vast amount of refuse.

As usual, the main course consisted of a piece of roast meat. Royal never asked about the source of the meat – dog, presumably. The women had the supply situation well in hand. Mrs Wilder stood beside him, gazing into the night air as Royal tasted the heavily spiced dish. Like a well-trained housekeeper, she was waiting for Royal to give some indication of approval, though she never seemed concerned by either praise or criticism. She spoke in a flat voice unlike the animated tone she used with Anne and the other women. In fact, Mrs Wilder spent more time with his wife than Royal did himself. Six women lived together in the adjacent apartment, ostensibly so that they could be more easily protected from a surprise attack. Sometimes Royal would visit Anne, but there was something daunting about the closely knit group of women, sitting on their beds surrounded by the garbage-sacks, together looking after the Wilder children. Their eyes would watch him as he hesitated in the door, waiting for him to go away. Even Anne had withdrawn from him, partly out of fear of Royal, but also because she realized that he no longer needed her. At last, after all the months of trying to maintain her superior status, Anne had decided to join her fellow residents.

'Good – it's excellent again. Wait ... before you go.' Royal put down his fork. Casually, he asked, 'Have you heard anything of him? Perhaps someone has seen him?'

Mrs Wilder shook her head, bored by this roundabout questioning. 'Who ...?'

'Your husband – Richard, I think he was called. *Wilder*.'

Mrs Wilder stared down at Royal, shaking her head as if not recognizing him. Royal was certain that she had not only forgotten the identity of her husband, but of all men, including himself. To test this, he placed his hand on her thigh, feeling the strong muscle. Mrs Wilder stood passively with her tray, unaware of Royal fondling her, partly because she had been molested by so many men during the past months, but also because the sexual assault itself had ceased to have any meaning. When Royal slipped two of his fingers into her natal cleft she reacted, not by pushing his hand away, but by moving it to her waist and lightly holding it there as she would the straying hands of her children.

When she had gone, taking the portion of meat which Royal always left for her, he sat back at the long table. He was glad to see her go. Without asking him, Mrs Wilder had laundered his white jacket, washing out the bloodstains which had given him not merely his sense of authority, but his whole unstated role within the high-rise.

Had she done this deliberately, knowing that it would emasculate him? Royal could still remember the period of endless parties, when the apartment building had been lit up like a drunken liner. Royal had played the role of feudal chief to the hilt, presiding each evening over the council meetings held in his drawing-room. As they sat together in the candlelight, these neurosurgeons, senior academics and stockbrokers displayed all the talents for intrigue and survival exercised by years of service in industry, commerce and university life. For all the formal vocabulary of agendas and minutes, proposed and seconded motions, the verbal paraphernalia bequeathed by a hundred committee meetings, these were in effect tribal conferences. Here they discussed the latest ruses for obtaining food and women, for defending the upper floors against marauders, their plans for alliance and betrayal. Now the new order had emerged, in which all life within the high-rise revolved around three obsessions – security, food and sex.

Leaving the table, Royal picked up a silver candlestick and carried it to the window. All the lights in the high-rise were out. Two floors, the 40th and the 37th, were left with electric current, but they remained unlit. The darkness was more comforting, a place where real illusions might flourish.

Forty floors below, a car turned into the parking-lot and threaded its way through the maze of access lanes to its place two hundred yards from the building. The driver, wearing a flying-jacket and heavy boots, stepped out and hurried head-down towards the entrance. Royal guessed that this unknown man was probably the last resident to leave the building and set off for his office. Whoever he was, he had found a route to and from his apartment.

Somewhere on the roof, a dog whimpered. Far below, from the mouth of an apartment twenty storeys down the cliff face, there was a brief isolated scream – whether of pain, lust or rage no longer mattered. Royal waited, his heart starting to race. A moment later there was a second scream, a meaningless wail. These cries were the expressions of totally abstracted emotions, detached from the context of events around them.

Royal waited, expecting one of his retinue to enter and inform him of the probable reasons for these disturbances. Apart from the women in the next apartment, several of the younger male residents – a gallery owner from the 39th floor, and a successful hairdresser from the 38th – usually lounged about in the corridor among the garbage-sacks, leaning on their spears and keeping an eye on the staircase barricades.

Picking up his chromium cane, Royal left the dining-room, a single candle in its silver stick lighting his way. As he stumbled over the black plastic bags he wondered why they had never heaved them over the side. Presumably they held this rubbish to themselves less from fear of attracting the attention of the outside world than from a need to cling to their own, surround themselves with the mucilage of unfinished meals, bloody bandage scraps, broken bottles that once held the wine that made them drunk, all faintly visible through the semi-opaque plastic.

His apartment was empty, the high-ceilinged rooms deserted. Cautiously, Royal stepped into the corridor. The guard-post by the barricades was unmanned, and no lights gleamed through the doorway of the adjacent apartment where the women lived. Surprised by the absence of light from the usually busy kitchen, Royal walked through the darkened hallway. He kicked aside a child's toy and raised the candlestick above his head, trying to pick out any sleeping human figures in the surrounding rooms.

Open suitcases lay on the mattresses that covered the floor of the master-bedroom. Royal stood in the doorway, a medley of scents crowding around him in the darkness, brilliant wakes left behind them by these fleeing women. Hesitating for a moment, he reached into the room and switched on the light.

The instant electric glow, so unfamiliar after the wavering candlelight and twitching torch-beams, shone down on the six mattresses in the room. Half-packed suitcases lay on top of each other, as if the women had left at a moment's notice, or at some prearranged signal. Most of their clothes had been left behind, and he recognized the trouser-suit which Mrs Wilder had worn to serve his dinner. The racks of Anne's dresses and suits hung in the wardrobes like a store display.

The even light, as dead as a time exposure in a police photograph recording a crime, lay across these torn mattresses and discarded clothes, the wine-stains on the walls and the forgotten cosmetics on the floor at his feet.

As Royal stared down at them, he could hear a faint hooting noise from the darkened corridor, moving away from him as if emitted by these escaping women. This series of whoops and nasal grunts he had been listening to for days, trying without success to repress them from his mind. Switching off the light, he seized his cane firmly in both hands and left the apartment.

Standing outside the door, he listened to the distant sounds, almost an electronic parody of a child's crying. They moved through the apartments at the far end of the floor, metallic and remote, the sounds of the beasts of his private zoo.

15

THE EVENING'S ENTERTAINMENT

The evening deepened, and the apartment building withdrew into the darkness. As usual at this hour, the high-rise was silent, as if everyone in the huge building was passing through a border zone. On the roof the dogs whimpered to themselves. Royal blew out the candles in the dining-room and made his way up the steps to the penthouse. Reflecting the distant lights of the neighbouring high-rises, the chromium shafts of the callisthenics machine seemed to move up and down like columns of mercury, a complex device recording the shifting psychological levels of the residents below. As Royal stepped on to the roof the darkness was lit by the white forms of hundreds of birds. Their wings flared in the dark air as they struggled to find a perch on the crowded elevator heads and balustrades.

Royal waited until they surrounded him, steering their beaks away from his legs with his stick. He felt himself becoming calm again. If the women and the other members of his dwindling entourage had decided to leave him, so much the better. Here in the darkness among the birds, listening to them swoop and cry, the dogs whimpering in the children's sculpture-garden, he felt most at home. He was convinced more than ever that the birds were attracted here by his own presence.

Royal scattered the birds out of his way and pushed back the gates of the sculpture-garden. As they recognized him, the dogs began to whine and strain, pulling against their leads. These retrievers, poodles and dachshunds were all that remained of the hundred or so animals who had once lived in the upper floors of the high-rise. They were kept here as a strategic food reserve, but Royal had seen to it that few of them had been eaten. The dogs formed his personal hunting pack, to be kept until the final confrontation when he would lead them down into the building, and throw open the windows of the barricaded apartments to admit the birds.

The dogs pulled at his legs, their leads entangled around the play-sculptures. Even Royal's favourite, the white Alsatian, was restless and on edge. Royal tried to settle it, running his hands over the luminous but still bloodstained coat. The dog butted him nervously, knocking him back across the empty food-pails.

As Royal regained his balance, he heard the sound of voices surging up the central stairway a hundred feet behind him. Lights approached through the darkness, a procession of electric torches held at shoulder height. The beams of light cut through the night air, scattering the birds into the sky. A portable cassette player boomed out its music over the clicking of dumb-bells. As Royal paused behind an elevator head, a group of his top-floor neighbours erupted on to the roof. Led by Pangbourne, they spread in a loose circle across the observation deck, ready to celebrate a recent triumph. Without Royal's approval or foreknowledge, a raid had taken place on the floors below.

The gynaecologist was in high excitement, waving the last stragglers up the staircase like a demented courier. From his mouth came a series of peculiar whoops and cries, barely articulated grunts that sounded like some Neanderthal mating call but, in fact, were Pangbourne's rendering of the recorded birth-cries analysed by his computer. These eerie and unsettling noises Royal had been forced to listen to for weeks as members of his entourage took up the refrain. A few days earlier he had finally banned the making of these noises altogether – sitting in the penthouse and trying to think about the birds, it unnerved him to hear the women in the kitchen next door emitting these clicks and grunts. However, Pangbourne held regular sessions in his own quarters at the opposite end of the roof, where he would play through his library of recorded birth-cries for the benefit of the women crouching in a hushed circle on the floor around him. Together they mimicked these weird noises, an oral emblem of Pangbourne's growing authority.

Now they had left Royal, and were giving full vent to everything they had learned, hooting and growling like a troupe of demented mothers-to-be invoking their infants' birth-traumas.

Waiting for the right moment to make his entrance, Royal heeled the Alsatian behind a tattered awning that leaned against the elevator head. For once he was glad that he was wearing his tuxedo – the white safari-jacket would have stood out like a flame.

Two 'guests' had been picked up, a cost-accountant from the 32nd floor with a bandaged head, and a myopic meteorologist from the 27th. The woman carrying the cassette player, he noted calmly, was his wife Anne. Sloppily dressed, her hair in a mess, she lolled against Pangbourne's shoulder and then wandered about in the circle of torchlight like a moody trollop, brandishing the cassette player at the two prisoners.

'Ladies … please, now. There's more to come.' Pangbourne calmed the women, his slim fingers like brittle sticks in the confused light. The portable bar was lifted upright. A table and two chairs were set beside it, and the guests uneasily took their seats. The cost-accountant was trying to straighten the unravelling bandage around his head, as if frightened that he might be called upon to play blind man's buff. The meteorologist squinted shortsightedly into the torchlight, hoping to recognize someone among those taking part in this revel. Royal knew everyone present, his neighbours of the past year, and could almost believe that he was attending one of the many cocktail parties held on the roof that summer. At the same time he felt that he was watching the opening act of a stylized opera or ballet, in which a restaurant is reduced to a single table and the doomed hero is taunted by a chorus of waiters, before being despatched to his death.

The hosts at this party had been drinking long before their two guests arrived. The jeweller's widow in the long fur coat, Anne with her cassette player, Jane Sheridan waving a cocktail shaker, all were lurching about as if to some deranged music only Royal was unable to hear.

Pangbourne called for quiet again. 'Now – keep our guests amused. They're looking bored. What are we playing tonight?'

A medley of suggestions was shouted out.

'Gang Plank!'

'Flying School, doctor!'

'Moon Walk!'

Pangbourne turned to his guests. 'I rather like Flying School … Did you know we've been running a flying school here? No—?'

'We've decided to offer you some free lessons,' Anne Royal told them.

'One free lesson,' Pangbourne corrected. Everyone sniggered at this. 'But that's all you'll need. Isn't it, Anne?'

'It's a remarkably effective course.'

'Solo first time, in fact.'

Already, led by the jeweller's widow, they were dragging the injured accountant towards the balustrade, everyone tripping over the bloodstained bandage unwrapping around his head. A pair of tattered papier-mâché wings, part of a child's angel costume, were fastened to the victim's back. The grunting and hooting began again.

Dragging the reluctant Alsatian after him, Royal stepped into view. Involved in their imminent execution, no one noticed him. As casually as he could muster, he called out, 'Pangbourne ...! Dr Pangbourne ...!'

The noise slackened. Torch-beams flicked through the darkness, whipping across Royal's silk-lapelled dinner-jacket, fixing on the white Alsatian trying to escape between his feet.

'Flying School! Flying School!' The sullen chant was taken up. Looking down at this unruly gang, Royal could almost believe that he was surrounded by a crowd of semi-literate children. The zoo had rebelled against its keeper.

Hearing Royal's voice, the gynaecologist turned from his prisoner, whose bandage he had expertly refastened. Wiping his hands, he strolled across the roof, almost mimicking Royal's casual saunter. But his eyes were examining Royal's face with a wholly professional curiosity, as if he had already decided that its expression of firm determination could be readjusted by cutting a minimum number of nerves and muscles.

The chant rose into the air. The torch-beams beat rhythmically across the darkness, striking Royal's face. He waited patiently for the clamour to subside. As Anne broke away from the crowd and ran forward he raised the chromium cane, ready to strike her. She stopped in front of him, smirking as she fluffed up her long skirt in a provocative gesture. Suddenly she turned the cassette player to full volume and thrust it into his face. A gabble of birth-cries filled the air.

'Royal ...' the jeweller's widow shouted warningly. 'Here's Wilder!'

Startled by the name, Royal flinched back, thrashing at the darkness with the chromium cane. The torch-beams swerved around him, the shadows of the overturned chairs swinging across the concrete roof. Expecting Wilder to lunge at him from behind, he stumbled across the awning and entangled himself in the dog's lead.

He heard laughter behind him. Controlling himself with an effort, he turned to face Pangbourne again. But the gynaecologist was walking away, looking back at him without hostility. He waved to Royal with a quick movement of his hand, as if flicking a dart at him, dismissing him for ever. The torches swung away from Royal, and everyone returned to the more serious business of tormenting the two guests.

Royal watched from the darkness as they argued over the prisoners. The confrontation with Pangbourne was over – or, more exactly, had never taken place. A simple ruse had unnerved him, leaving him with the uncertainty of whether or not he really feared Wilder. He had been humiliated, but in a sense this was only just. The gynaecologist was the man for their hour. No zoo would survive for long with Pangbourne as its keeper, but he would provide a node of violence and cruelty that would keep alive in others the will to survive.

Let the psychotics take over. They alone understood what was happening. Holding to the Alsatian, Royal let the dog drag him away towards the safety of the darkness near the sculpture-garden. The white forms of the birds were massed together on every ledge and parapet. Royal listened to the whimpering dogs. He had no means now of feeding them. The glass doors of the penthouse reflected the swerving birds, like the casements of a secret pavilion. He would close down his apartment, block the staircase and retreat to the penthouse, perhaps taking Mrs Wilder with him as his servant. Here he would preside over the high-rise, taking up his last tenancy in the sky.

He unlocked the gate of the sculpture-garden and moved through the darkness among the statues, releasing the dogs. One by one they scrambled away, until only Royal and the birds were left.

16

A HAPPY ARRANGEMENT

An uncertain scene, Robert Laing decided. He could no longer trust his senses. A curious light, grey and humid but at the same time marbled by a faint interior luminosity, hung over the apartment. As he stood among the garbage-sacks in the kitchen, trying to coax a few drops of water from the tap, he peered over his shoulder at the dull fog that stretched like a curtain across the sitting-room, almost an extension of his own mind. Not for the first time he was unsure what time of day it was. How long had he been up? Laing vaguely remembered sleeping on the tartan rug that lay on the kitchen floor, his head pillowed on a garbage-sack between the table legs. He had been wandering about the bedroom where his sister Alice lay asleep, but whether he had woken five minutes ago or the previous day Laing had no means of telling.

He shook his watch, picking at the fractured dial with a grimy finger-nail. The watch had stopped during a scuffle in the 25th-floor lobby several days earlier. Although he had forgotten the exact moment, the hands of this broken watch contained the one point of finite time left to him, like a fossil cast on to a beach, crystallizing for ever a brief sequence of events within a vanished ocean. However, it barely mattered now what time it was – anything rather than night, when it was too terrifying to do more than shelter in the apartment, crouching behind his dilapidated barricade.

Laing turned the cold water tap on and off, listening to the faintly changing tone. At rare intervals, perhaps for a single minute during the day, a green, algae-stained liquid flowed from the tap. These small columns of water, moving up and down the huge system of pipes that ran throughout the building, announced their arrivals and departures with faint changes of note. Listening to this remote and complex music had sharpened Laing's ears, a sensitivity that extended to almost any kind of sound within the building. By contrast his sight, dulled by being used chiefly at night, presented him with an increasingly opaque world.

Little movement took place within the high-rise. As Laing often reminded himself, almost everything that could happen had already taken place. He left the kitchen and squeezed himself into the narrow niche between the front door and the barricade. He placed his right ear to the sounding panel of the wooden door. From the minute reverberations he could tell instantly if a marauder was moving through the abandoned apartments nearby. During the brief period each afternoon when he and Steele emerged from their apartments – a token remembrance of that time when people had actually left the building – they would take turns standing with their hands pressed against the metal walls of an elevator shaft, feeling the vibrations transmitted to their bodies, picking up a sudden movement fifteen floors above or below. Crouched on the staircase with their fingers on the metal rails, they listened to the secret murmurs of the building, the distant spasms of violence that communicated themselves like bursts of radiation from another universe. The high-rise quivered with these tremors, sinister trickles of sound as a wounded tenant crawled up a stairway, a trap closed around a wild dog, an unwary prey went down before a club.

Today, however, befitting this timeless zone with its uncertain light, there was no sound at all. Laing returned to the kitchen and listened to the water-pipes, part of a huge acoustic system operated by thousands of stops, this dying musical instrument they had once all played together. But everything was quiet. The residents of the high-rise remained where they were, hiding behind the barricades in their apartments, conserving what was left of their sanity and preparing themselves for the night. By now what violence there was had become totally stylized, spasms of cold and random aggression. In a sense life in the high-rise had begun to resemble the world outside – there were the same ruthlessness and aggression concealed within a set of polite conventions.

Still uncertain how long he had been awake, or what he had been doing half an hour earlier, Laing sat down among the empty bottles and refuse on the kitchen floor. He gazed up at the derelict washing-machine and refrigerator, now only used as garbage-bins. He found it hard to remember what their original function had been. To some extent they had taken on a new significance, a role that he had yet to understand. Even the run-down nature of the high-rise was a model of the world into which the future was carrying them, a landscape beyond technology where everything was either derelict or, more ambiguously, recombined in unexpected but more meaningful ways. Laing pondered this – sometimes he found it difficult not to believe that they were living in a future that had already taken place, and was now exhausted.

Squatting beside his dried-up water-hole like a desert nomad with all the time in the world, Laing waited patiently for the taps to flow. He picked at the dirt on the backs of his hands. Despite his tramp-like appearance he dismissed the notion of using the water to wash. The high-rise stank. None of the lavatories or garbage-disposal chutes were working, and a faint spray of urine hung over the face of the building, drifting across the tiers of balconies. Overlaying this characteristic odour, however, was a far more ambiguous smell, putrid and sweet, that tended to hover around empty apartments, and which Laing chose not to investigate too closely.

For all its inconveniences, Laing was satisfied with life in the high-rise. Now that so many of the residents were out of the way he felt able to relax, more in charge of himself and ready to move forward and explore his life. How and where exactly, he had not yet decided.

His real concern was with his sister. Alice had fallen ill with a non-specific malaise, and spent her time lying on the mattress in Laing's bedroom or wandering half-naked around the apartment, her body shuddering like an over-sensitive seismograph at imperceptible tremors that shook the building. When Laing drummed on the waste-pipe below the sink, sending a hollow drone through the empty pipe, Alice called out from the bedroom in her thin voice.

Laing went in to see her, picking his way among the piles of kindling he had made from chopped-up furniture. He enjoyed cutting up the chairs and tables.

Alice pointed to him with a stick-like hand. 'The noise – you're signalling again to someone. Who is it now?'

'No one, Alice. Who do you think we know?'

'Those people on the lower floors. The ones you like.'

Laing stood beside her, uncertain whether to sit on the mattress. His sister's face was as greasy as a wax lemon. Trying to focus on him, her tired eyes drifted about in her head like lost fish. It crossed his mind briefly that she might be dying – during the past two days they had eaten no more than a few fillets of canned smoked salmon, which he had found under the floorboards in an empty apartment. Ironically, the standard of cuisine in the apartment building had begun to rise during these days of its greatest decline, as more and more delicacies came to light.

However, food was a secondary matter, and Alice was very much alive in other ways. Laing enjoyed her wheedling criticisms of him, as he tried to satisfy her pointless whims. All this was a game, but he relished the role of over-dutiful servant dedicated to a waspish mistress, a devoted menial whose chief satisfaction was a total lack of appreciation and the endless recitation of his faults. In many ways, in fact, his relationship with Alice recapitulated that which his wife had unthinkingly tried to create, hitting by accident on the one possible source of harmony between them, and which Laing had rejected at the time. Within the high-rise, he reflected, his marriage would have succeeded triumphantly.

'I'm trying to find some water, Alice. You'd like a little tea?'

'The kettle smells.'

'I'll wash it for you. You mustn't become dehydrated.'

She nodded grudgingly. 'What's been happening?'

'Nothing … It's already happened.' A ripe but not unpleasant smell rose from Alice's body. 'Everything is starting to get back to normal.'

'What about Alan – you said you'd look for him.'

'I'm afraid he's gone.' Laing disliked these references to Alice's husband. They introduced a discordant note. 'I found your apartment but it's empty now.'

Alice turned her head away, indicating that she had seen enough of her brother. Laing bent down and gathered together the kindling she had scattered on the floor beside the mattress. These dining-room chair-legs, well impregnated with glue and varnish, would burn briskly. Laing had looted the chairs from Adrian Talbot's apartment after the psychiatrist's disappearance. He was grateful for this reproduction Hepplewhite – the conventional tastes of the middle-floor residents had served them well. By contrast, those on the lower levels found themselves with a clutter of once-fashionable chromium tubing and undressed leather, useless for anything but sitting on.

All cooking was now done over fires which the residents lit for themselves on their balconies, or in the artificial fireplaces. Laing carried the sticks on to the balcony. As he squatted there he realized that he had nothing to cook. The secret cache of cans he had long ago been obliged to surrender to the orthodontic surgeon next door. In fact, Laing's position was secure thanks only to the morphine ampoules he had concealed.

Although Steele frightened him with his unpredictable cruelties, Laing had attached himself to him out of necessity. So many people had gone, or dropped out of the struggle altogether. Had they deserted the high-rise for the world outside? Laing was sure that they had not. In a sense he depended on the uncertainties of his relationship with the dentist, following his murderous swings like a condemned prisoner in love with a moody jailer. During the previous weeks Steele's behaviour had become frightening. The deliberately mindless assaults on anyone found alone or unprotected, the infantile smearing of blood on the walls of empty apartments – all these Laing watched uneasily. Since his wife's disappearance Steele had been as tautly strung as the huge crossbows which he constructed from piano wire and mounted in the lobbies and corridors, their vicious arrows fashioned from the shafts of golf-clubs. At the same time, however, Steele remained strangely calm, as if pursuing some unknown quest.

Steele slept in the afternoon, giving Laing a chance to prospect for water. As he picked up the kettle he heard Alice call out to him, but when he returned to her she had already forgotten what she wanted.

She held out her hands to him. Usually Laing would have rubbed them for her, trying to kindle a little warmth in them, but out of some kind of peculiar loyalty to the dentist he made no effort to help Alice. This petty show of callousness, his declining personal hygiene, and even his deliberate neglect of his health, were elements in a system he made no attempt to change. For weeks all he had been able to think about were the next raid, the next apartment to be ransacked, the next tenant to be beaten up. He enjoyed watching Steele at work, obsessed with these expressions of mindless violence. Each one brought them a step closer to the ultimate goal of the high-rise, a realm where their most deviant impulses were free at last to exercise themselves in any way they wished. At this point physical violence would cease at last.

Laing waited for Alice to subside into half-consciousness. Looking after his sister was taking up more of his energy than he could afford. If she was dying there was little he could do, apart from giving her a terminal gram of morphine and hiding her body before Steele could mutilate it. Dressing up corpses and setting them in grotesque tableaux was a favourite pastime of the dentist's. His imagination, repressed by all the years of reconstructing his patients' mouths, came alive particularly when he was playing with the dead. The previous day Laing had blundered into an apartment and found him painting a bizarre cosmetic mask on the face of a dead account-executive, dressing the body like an overblown drag-queen in a voluminous silk nightdress. Given time, and a continuing supply of subjects, the dentist would repopulate the entire high-rise.

Carrying the kettle, Laing let himself out of the apartment. The same dim light, pearled by a faint interior glow, filled the corridor and elevator lobby, a miasma secreted by the high-rise itself, distillation of all its dead concrete. The walls were spattered with blood, overlaying the aerosolled graffiti like the tachist explosions in the paintings that filled the top-floor apartments. Broken furniture and unravelled recording tape lay among the garbage-sacks piled against the walls.

Laing's feet crackled among the polaroid negatives scattered about the corridor floor, each recording a long-forgotten act of violence. As he paused, wary of attracting the attention of a watching predator, the staircase doors opened and a man in a flying-jacket and fleece-lined boots entered the lobby.

Watching Paul Crosland stride purposefully across the debris-strewn carpet, Laing realized that the television announcer had just returned, as he did every day, from reading the lunch-time news bulletin at the television station. Crosland was the only person to leave the high-rise, maintaining a last tenuous link with the outside world. Even Steele side-stepped him discreetly. A few people still watched him read the news on their battery-powered sets, crouching among the garbage-sacks behind their barricades, perhaps still hoping that even now Crosland might suddenly depart from his set text and blurt out to the world at large what was happening within the high-rise.

Inside the staircase Laing had set up a dog trap, using a tropical mosquito-net he had lifted from an anthropologist's apartment three floors above. A plague of dogs had descended the building from their breeding grounds on the upper floors. Laing had no hopes of catching the larger dogs in the spring-loaded contraption, but a dachshund or pekinese might become entangled in the nylon mesh.

The staircase was unguarded. Taking a chance, Laing made his way down the steps to the floor below. The lobby was blocked by a barricade of furniture, and he turned into the corridor that served the ten apartments in the northern wing of the building.

Three doors along, he entered an abandoned apartment. The rooms were empty, the furniture and fittings long since stripped away. In the kitchen Laing tried the taps. With his sheath-knife he cut the hoses of the washing-machine and dishwasher, collecting a cupful of metallic water. In the bathroom the naked body of an elderly tax-specialist lay on the tiled floor. Without thinking, Laing stepped over him. He wandered around the apartment, picking up an empty whisky decanter on the floor. A faint odour of malt whisky clung to it, an almost intoxicating nostalgia.

Laing moved to the next apartment, also abandoned and gutted. In a bedroom he noticed that the carpet covered a small circular depression. Suspecting a secret food cache, he rolled back the carpet, and found that a manhole had been drilled through the wooden floorboards and concrete deck to the apartment below.

After sealing the door, Laing lay down on the floor and peered into the room beneath. A circular glass table, by a miracle still intact, reflected his blood-spattered shirt and bearded face, staring up from what seemed to be the bottom of a deep well. Beside the table were two overturned armchairs. The balcony doors were closed, and curtains hung on either side of the windows. Looking down at this placid scene, Laing felt that he had accidentally been given a glimpse into a parallel world, where the laws of the high-rise were suspended, a magical domain where these huge buildings were furnished and decorated but never occupied.

On an impulse, Laing eased his thin legs through the manhole. He sat on the ledge and swung himself down into the room below. Standing on the glass table, he surveyed the apartment. Hard experience told him that he was not alone – somewhere a miniature bell was ringing. A faint scratching came from the bedroom, as if a small animal was trying to escape from a paper sack.

Laing pushed back the bedroom door. A red-haired woman in her mid-thirties lay fully dressed on the bed, playing with a Persian cat. The creature wore a velvet collar and bell, and its lead was attached to the woman's bloodied wrist. The cat vigorously licked at the bloodstains on its coat, and then seized the woman's wrist and gnawed at the thin flesh, trying to reopen a wound.

The woman, whom Laing vaguely recognized as Eleanor Powell, made no effort to stop the cat from dining off her flesh. Her serious face, with its blue cyanosed hue, was inclined over the cat like that of a tolerant parent watching a child at play.

Her left hand lay across the silk bedspread, touching a pencil and reporter's note-pad. Facing her, at the foot of the bed, were four television sets. They were tuned to different stations, but three of the screens were blank. On the fourth, a battery-powered set, the out-of-focus picture of a horserace was being projected soundlessly.

Uninterested in her reviewing, Eleanor teased her bloodied wrist into the cat's mouth. The creature was ravenous, tearing excitedly at the flesh around the knuckle. Laing tried to pull the cat away, but Eleanor jerked at the lead, urging it back on to her wound.

'I'm keeping her alive,' she told Laing reprovingly. The cat's attentions brought a serene smile to her face. She raised her left hand. 'Doctor, you may suckle my other wrist … Poor man, you look thin enough.'

Laing listened to the sounds of the cat's teeth. The apartment was silent, and the noise of his own excited breathing was magnified to an uncanny extent. Would he soon be the last person alive in the high-rise? He thought of himself in this enormous building, free to roam its floors and concrete galleries, to climb its silent elevator shafts, to sit by himself in turn on every one of its thousand balconies. This dream, longed for since his arrival at the high-rise, suddenly unnerved him, almost as if, at last alone here, he had heard footsteps in the next room and come face to face with himself.

He turned up the volume of the television set. A racetrack commentator's voice emerged from the speaker, a gabble of names that sounded like a demented inventory, a list of unrelated objects being recruited to repopulate the high-rise in an emergency transfusion of identity.

'What—? Where's the programme?' Eleanor raised her head, peering disjointedly at the television set. Her left hand scrabbled around for the dictation pad and pencil. 'What's he saying?'

Laing slipped his arms under her. He intended to carry her, but her thin body was surprisingly heavy. He was weaker than he had thought. 'Can you walk? I'll come back later for the set.'

She shrugged vaguely, swaying against Laing like a drunk in a bar accepting a dubious proposition from an old acquaintance. Sitting beside him on the edge of the bed, she leaned an arm on his shoulder, inspecting him with a shrewd eye. She tapped Laing aggressively on the arm. 'All right. First thing, though, find some batteries.'

'Of course.' Her show of wilfulness was pleasantly encouraging. As she watched from the bed he pulled a suitcase from the wardrobe and began to fill it with her clothes.

So Laing took Eleanor Powell and her portable television set back to his apartment. He arranged her on a mattress in the living-room, and spent his days hunting the abandoned apartments for food, water and batteries. The reappearance of television in his life convinced Laing that everything in the high-rise was becoming normal again. When Steele moved on to the richer pastures above, Laing declined his offer to join him. Already Laing had decided to separate himself and his two women from everyone else. He needed to be alone with Alice and Eleanor, to be as aggressive and self-reliant, as passive and submissive as he wished. He had little idea at this early stage of what role he would play with these two women, but whatever he chose he would have to play out within his own walls.

Laing knew that he was far happier now than ever before, despite all the hazards of his life, the likelihood that he would die at any time from hunger or assault. He was satisfied by his self-reliance, his ability to cope with the tasks of survival – foraging, keeping his wits about him, guarding his two women from any marauder who might want to use them for similar purposes. Above all, he was pleased with his good sense in giving rein to those impulses that involved him with Eleanor and his sister, perversities created by the limitless possibilities of the high rise.

17

THE LAKESIDE PAVILION

As if nervous of disturbing the interior of the apartment building, the morning sun explored the half-shuttered skylight of the 40th floor stairwell, slipped between the broken panes and fell obliquely down the steps. Shivering in the cold air five floors below, Richard Wilder watched the sunlight approach him. He sat on the steps, leaning against a dining-room table which formed part of a massive barricade blocking the staircase. After crouching here all night, Wilder was frozen. The higher up the building he moved, the colder it became, and at times he had been tempted to retreat to the floors below. He looked down at the animal crouching beside him – a black poodle, he guessed it had once been – envying its shaggy coat. His own body was almost naked, and he rubbed at the lipstick smeared across his chest and shoulders, trying to insulate himself with this sweet grease.

The dog's eyes were fixed on the landing above. Its ears pricked as it detected the sounds, inaudible to Wilder, of someone moving behind the barricade. During their ten days together the two had formed a successful hunting team, and Wilder was reluctant to urge the dog to attack before it was ready.

The threadbare remains of Wilder's trousers, cut away at the knees, were stained with blood and wine. A ragged beard covered his heavy face, partly concealing an open wound on his jaw. He looked derelict and exhausted, but in fact his body was as strongly muscled as ever. His broad chest was covered with a hatchwork of painted lines, a vivid display that spread across his shoulders and back. At intervals he inspected the design, which he had painted the previous afternoon with a lipstick he had found in an abandoned apartment. What had begun as a drink-fuddled game had soon taken on a serious ritual character. The markings, apart from frightening the few other people he might come across, gave him a potent sense of identity. As well, they celebrated his long and now virtually successful ascent of the high-rise. Determined to look his best when he finally stepped on to the roof, Wilder licked his scarred fingers, massaging himself with one hand and freshening up his design with the other.

He held the dog's leash in a strong grip and watched the landing ten steps above him. The sun, continuing its laboured descent of the stairwell, at last reached him and began to warm his skin. Wilder looked up at the skylight sixty feet above his head. The rectangle of white sky became more and more unreal as it drew closer, like the artificial ceiling of a film set.

The dog quivered, edging its paws forwards. Only a few yards from them, someone was straightening part of the barricade. Wilder waited patiently, moving the dog up one step. For all the savage-like ferocity of his appearance, Wilder's behaviour was a model of restraint. Having come this far, he had no intention of being caught unawares. He peered through a crack in the dining-table. Behind the barricade someone pulled back a small mahogany writing-desk that served as a concealed door. Through this gap appeared an almost bald woman of about seventy. Her tough face peered into the stairwell. After a wary pause, she stepped through the gap to the landing rail, a champagne bucket in one hand. She was dressed in the remnants of an expensive evening gown, which exposed the mottled white skin of her muscular arms and shoulders.

Wilder watched her with respect. He had tangled with these crones more than once, and was well aware that they were capable of a surprising turn of speed. Without moving, he waited as she leaned over the landing rail and emptied the slops from the champagne bucket. The cold grease spattered Wilder and the dog, but neither made any response. Wilder carefully wiped the cine-camera lying on the step beside him. Its lenses had been fractured during the skirmishes and assaults that had brought him to the roof of the high-rise, but the camera's role was now wholly emblematic. He felt the same identification with the camera that he did with the dog. However, for all his affection and loyalty towards the animal, the dog would soon be leaving him – they would both be present at a celebratory dinner when they reached the roof, he reflected with a touch of gallows-humour, but the poodle would be in the pot.

Thinking of this supper to come – his first decent meal for weeks – Wilder watched the old woman muttering about. He wiped his beard, and cautiously raised himself from his knees. He pulled the dog's lead, a length of electric cord, and hissed between his broken teeth.

As if on cue, the dog whimpered. It stood up, shivering, and climbed two steps. In full view of the old woman it crouched down and began to whine plaintively. The old woman retreated swiftly behind her barricade. Within seconds a heavy carving-knife materialized in her hand. Her canny eyes peered down at the dog cringing on the steps below her. As it rolled on to its side and exposed its loins her eyes were riveted on its fleshy stomach and shoulders.

As the dog whimpered again, Wilder watched from behind the dining-table. This moment never failed to amuse him. In fact, the higher he climbed the building, the greater its potential for humour. He still held the lead, which trailed behind the dog down the steps, but was careful to leave it loose. The old woman, unable to take her eyes off the dog, stepped through the gap in the barricade. She whistled through the gap in her false teeth, and beckoned the dog forward.

'Poor pet. You're lost, aren't you, beauty? Come on, up here ...'

Barely able to contain his glee at the spectacle of this bald-headed crone fawning with exaggerated pathos over the dog, Wilder leaned against the table, laughing soundlessly to himself. At any moment she would be in for a shock, his heavy boot on her neck.

Behind the barricade a second figure appeared. A young woman of about thirty, probably the daughter, peered over the old woman's shoulder. Her suede jacket was unbuttoned to reveal a pair of grimy breasts, but her hair was elaborately wound into a mass of rollers, as if she were preparing parts of her body for some formal gala to which the rest of herself had not been invited.

The two women stared down at the dog, their faces expressionless. As the daughter waited with the carving-knife the mother edged down the steps. Muttering reassuringly, she patted the poodle on the head and bent down to take the lead.

As her strong fingers closed around the cord Wilder leapt forward. The dog sprang to life, hurled itself up the steps and sank its teeth into the old woman's arm. With surprising agility, she darted through the gap in the barricade, the dog clamped to her arm. Barely in time, Wilder followed her, kicking back the writing-desk before the daughter could lock it into place. He dragged the poodle from the old woman's bloodied arm, seized her by the neck and flung her sideways across a stack of cardboard cartons. She lay there stunned, like a dishevelled duchess surprised to find herself drunk at a ball. As Wilder turned away, wrestling with the dog, the daughter ran towards him. She had thrown the carving-knife aside. In one hand she held her hair curlers, in the other a silver handbag pistol. Wilder side-stepped out of her way, knocked the pistol from her hand and clubbed her backwards across the barricade.

As the two women sat panting on the floor, Wilder looked down at the pistol at his feet, little more than a child's bright toy. He picked it up and began to inspect his new domain. He was standing in the entrance to the 35th-floor swimming-pool. The tank of foetid water, filled with debris, reflected the garbage-sacks heaped around the tiled verge. A small den had been built inside a stationary elevator in the lobby. Beside a burnt-out fire an elderly man – a former tax-consultant, Wilder seemed to recall – lay asleep, apparently unaware of the spasm of violence that had taken place. A chimney flue, fashioned from two lengths of balcony drainage pipe, exited over his head through the roof of the elevator.

Still holding the pistol, Wilder watched the two women. The mother sat among the cardboard cartons, matter-of-factly bandaging her arm with a strip torn from her silk dress. The daughter squatted on the floor by the barricade, rubbing the bruise on her mouth and patting the head of Wilder's poodle.

Wilder peered up the staircase to the 36th floor. The skirmish had excited him, and he was tempted to press on all the way to the roof. However, he had not eaten for more than a day, and the smell of animal fat hung in the air around the fire by the entrance to the den.

Wilder beckoned the young woman towards him. Her bland, rather bovine face was vaguely familiar. Had she once been the wife of a film-company executive? She climbed to her feet and walked up to him, staring with interest at the emblems painted across his chest and shoulders, and at his exposed genitals. Pocketing the pistol, Wilder pulled her towards the den. They stepped over the old man and entered the elevator. Curtains hung from the walls, and two mattresses covered the floor. Holding the young woman to him, an arm around her shoulders, Wilder sat down against the rear wall of the elevator. He gazed across the lobby at the yellow water of the swimming-pool. Several of the changing cubicles had been converted into small, single-tenant cabins, but they were all now abandoned. Two bodies, he noted, floated in the pool, barely distinguishable from the other debris, the kitchen garbage and pieces of furniture.

Wilder helped himself to the last of the small cat that had been barbecued above the fire. His teeth pulled at the stringy meat, the still warm fat almost intoxicating him as he sucked at the skewer.

The young woman leaned affably against him, content to have Wilder's strong arm around her shoulders. The fresh smell of her body surprised him – the higher up the apartment building he moved the cleaner were the women. Wilder looked down at her unmarked face, as open and amiable as a domestic animal's. She seemed to have been totally untouched by events within the high-rise, as if waiting in some kind of insulated chamber for Wilder to appear. He tried to speak to her, but found himself grunting, unable to form the words with his broken teeth and scarred tongue.

Pleasantly high on the meat, he lay back comfortably against the young woman, playing with the silver handbag pistol. Without thinking, he opened the front of her suede jacket and loosened her breasts. He placed his hands over the small nipples and settled himself against her. He felt drowsy, murmuring to the young woman while she stroked the painted stripes on his chest and shoulders, her fingers moving endlessly across his skin as if writing a message to him.

Lying back in this comfortable lakeside pavilion Wilder rested during the early afternoon. The young woman sat beside him, her breasts against his face, nursing this huge, nearly naked man with his painted body and exposed loins. Her mother and father pottered about in the lobby. Now and then the old woman in her evening gown pulled a piece of furniture at random from the barricade and chopped it into kindling with the carving knife.

Wilder ignored them, conscious only of the young woman's body and the huge pillars that carried the apartment building upwards to the roof. Through the windows around the swimming-pool he could see the towers of the four high-rise blocks nearby, suspended like rectilinear clouds within the afternoon sky. The warmth within the elevator, which seemed to emanate from the young woman's breasts, had drained all will and energy from him. Her calm face gazed down at Wilder reassuringly. She had accepted him as she would any marauding hunter. First she would try to kill him, but failing this give him food and her body, breast-feed him back to a state of childishness and even, perhaps, feel affection for him. Then, the moment he was asleep, cut his throat. The synopsis of the ideal marriage.

Rallying himself, Wilder sat up and put his boot into the poodle lying asleep on the mattress outside the elevator. The yelp of pain revived Wilder. He pushed the young woman away. He needed to sleep, but first he would move to a safer hiding-place, or the crone and her daughter would make short work of him.

Without looking back, he stood up and dragged the dog behind him. He slipped the silver pistol into the waistband of his trousers and checked the patterns on his chest and shoulders. Carrying the cine-camera, he climbed past the barricade and re-entered the staircase, leaving behind the quiet encampment and the young woman beside her yellow lake.

As he moved up the steps everything was silent. The staircase was carpeted, muffling the tread of his boots, and he was too distracted by the sounds of his own breathing to notice that the walls around him had been freshly painted, their white surfaces gleaming in the afternoon sunlight like the entrance to an abattoir.

Wilder climbed to the 37th floor, smelling the icy air moving across his naked body from the open sky. He could hear now, more clearly than ever before, the crying of gulls. When the dog began to whimper, reluctant to go any further, he turned it loose, and watched it disappear down the stairs.

The 37th floor was deserted, apartment doors open on the bright air. Too exhausted to think, he found an empty apartment, barricaded himself into the living-room and sank into a deep sleep on the floor.

18

THE BLOOD GARDEN

By contrast, Anthony Royal, high on the open roof three floors above, had never been more awake. Ready at last to join the sea-birds, he stood at the windows of his penthouse, looking out over the open plazas of the development project towards the distant mouth of the river. Washed by the recent rain, the morning air was clear but frozen, and the river flowed from the city like a stream of ice. For two days Royal had eaten nothing, but far from exhausting him the absence of food had stimulated every nerve and muscle in his body. The shrieking of the gulls filled the air, and seemed to tear at the exposed tissues of his brain. They rose from the elevator heads and balustrades in a continuous fountain, soared into the air to form an expanding vortex and dived down again towards the sculpture-garden.

Royal was certain now that they were calling for him. He had been deserted by the dogs – as soon as he freed them they had disappeared into the stairways and corridors below – and only the white Alsatian remained. It sat at Royal's feet by the open windows, mesmerized by the movement of the birds. Its wounds had healed now, and its thick arctic coat was white again. Royal missed the stains, as he did the bloody hand-prints that Mrs Wilder had washed from his jacket.

The little food Royal had taken with him before sealing himself into the penthouse he had given to the dog, but already he felt himself beyond hunger. For three days he had seen no one, and was glad to have cut himself off from his wife and neighbours. Looking up at the whirling cloud of gulls, he knew that they were the true residents of the high-rise. Without realizing it at the time, he had designed the sculpture-garden for them alone.

Royal shivered in the cold air. He wore his safari-jacket, and the thin linen gave him no protection against the wind moving across the concrete roof. In the over-lit air the white fabric was grey by comparison with Royal's chalk-like skin. Barely able to control himself, and uncertain whether the scars of his accident had begun to reopen themselves, he stepped on to the terrace and walked across the roof.

The gulls sidled around him, rolling their heads and wiping their beaks against the concrete. The surface was streaked with blood. For the first time Royal saw that the ledges and balustrades were covered with these bloody notches, the symbols of a mysterious calligraphy.

Voices sounded in the distance, a murmur of women. In the central section of the observation deck, beyond the sculpture-garden, a group of women residents had gathered for some kind of public discussion.

Unsettled by this intrusion into his private landscape, and its reminder that he was not yet alone in the apartment building, Royal retreated behind the rear wall of the sculpture-garden. The voices moved around him, talking away informally as if this were the latest of many similar visits. Perhaps he had been asleep during their previous excursions, or with the cooler weather they had decided to move their meeting place further along the roof to the shelter of his penthouse.

The vortex of birds was breaking up. As Royal returned to the penthouse the spiral had begun to disintegrate. The gulls dived away across the face of the building far below. Urging the Alsatian ahead of him, Royal emerged from behind the rear wall of the sculpture-garden. Two of the women were standing inside the penthouse, one of them with a hand on the callisthenics machine. What startled Royal was their casual stance, as if they were about to move into a vacation villa they had recently rented.

Royal retreated behind an elevator head. After being alone with the birds and the white Alsatian for so long the sight of these human intruders unsettled him. He pulled the dog against his legs, deciding to wait in the sculpture-garden until the visiting party had left.

He pushed back the rear door of the garden, and walked between the painted geometric forms. Dozens of the gulls surrounded him, crowded together on the tiled floor. They followed Royal expectantly, almost as if they had been waiting for him to bring something to them.

His feet slipped on the wet tiles. Looking down, he found a piece of gristle attached to his shoe. Pulling it away, he leaned against one of the concrete sculptures, a waist-high sphere that had been painted bright carmine.

When he drew his hand away it was wet with blood. As the birds strutted ahead, clearing an open space for him, he saw that the whole interior of the play-garden was drenched with blood. The tiled floor was slick with bright mucilage.

The Alsatian snuffled greedily, wolfing down a shred of flesh lying by the edge of the paddling pool. Appalled, Royal stared at the blood-spattered tiles, at his bright hands, at the white bones picked clean by the birds.

It was late afternoon when Wilder woke. Cold air moved through the empty room, flicking at a newspaper on the floor. The apartment was without shadows. Wilder listened to the wind moving down the ventilation shafts. The screaming of the gulls had ended, as if the birds had gone away for ever. Wilder sat on the floor in a corner of the living-room, an apex of this untenanted cube. Feeling the pressure of his back against the wall, he could almost believe that he was the first and last occupant of this apartment building.

He climbed to his feet and walked across the floor to the balcony. Far below, he could see the thousands of cars in the parking-lots, but they were screened from him by a faint mist, part of the corroborative detail of a world other than his own.

Sucking at the traces of animal fat that clung to his fingers, Wilder entered the kitchen. The cupboards and refrigerator were empty. He thought of the young woman and her warm body in the elevator beside the pool, wondering whether to go back to her. He remembered her stroking his chest and shoulders, and could feel the pressure of her hands on his skin.

Still sucking his fingers, and thinking of himself abandoned in this huge building, Wilder stepped out of the apartment. The corridor was silent, the cold air stirring the tags of refuse on the floor. He carried the cine-camera in his left hand, but he was no longer certain what its function was, or why he had kept it with him for so long.

The silver pistol, by contrast, he recognized immediately. He held it in his right hand, pointing it playfully at the open doorways, and half-hoping that someone would come out to join him in his game. The top floors of the building had been partially invaded by the sky. He saw white clouds through an elevator shaft, framed in the skylight of the stairwell as he climbed to the 40th floor.

Feinting with the pistol, Wilder darted across the elevator lobby of the 40th floor. There were no barricades here, and a recent attempt had been made at housekeeping. The garbage-sacks had been removed, the barricades dismantled, the lobby furniture re-installed. Someone had scrubbed the walls, clearing away all traces of the graffiti, duty rosters and elevator embarkation times.

Behind him, a door closed in the wind, cutting off a shaft of light. Enjoying this game with himself in the empty building, and certain that someone would soon turn up to play with him, Wilder dropped to one knee and levelled the pistol at an imaginary assailant. He darted down the corridor, kicked back the door and burst into the apartment.

The apartment was the largest he had seen in the building, far more spacious than any others on the upper floors. Like the lobby and corridor, the rooms had been carefully cleaned, the carpets re-laid, the curtains hung around the high windows. On the polished dining-room table stood two silver candlesticks.

Impressed by this sight, Wilder wandered around the gleaming table. In some confused way he felt that he had already been here, many years before he came to this empty building. The high ceiling and masculine furniture reminded him of a house he had visited as a small child. He wandered around the refurnished rooms, almost expecting to find his childhood toys, a cot and playpen laid out for his arrival.

Between the bedrooms a private staircase led upwards to another chamber, and a small suite of rooms overlooking the roof. Excited by the mystery and challenge of this secret staircase, Wilder began to climb the steps. Licking the last of the fat from his fingers, he trumpeted happily to himself.

He was half-way up the staircase, climbing towards the open air, when something blocked his path. The gaunt figure of a tall, white-haired man had stepped forward from the shadows. Far older than Wilder, his hair dishevelled by the wind, he stood at the head of the staircase, looking down silently at the intruder below him. His face was concealed by the harsh light, but the scars on the bony points of his forehead stood out clearly, like the fresh hand-stains that marked his white jacket.

Dimly recognizing this wild old man of the observation roof, Wilder stopped on the stairs. He was unsure whether Royal had come to play with him or to reprimand him. From Royal's nervous posture, and his destitute appearance, Wilder guessed that he had been hiding somewhere, but not as part of a game.

Hoping none the less to enlist him, Wilder waved his pistol playfully at Royal. To his surprise the architect flinched back, as if pretending to be frightened. As Wilder climbed towards him he raised the chromium cane in his hand and hurled it down the staircase.

The metal rod struck the hand-rail and whipped across Wilder's left arm. Stung by the pain of the blow, Wilder dropped the cine-camera. His arm was numb, and for a moment he felt helpless, like an abused child. As the architect advanced down the steps towards him, Wilder raised the silver pistol and shot him through the chest.

When the brief explosion had faded across the cold air, Wilder climbed the last of the steps. The architect's body lay awkwardly across the staircase, as if he were pretending to be dead. His scarred face, drained of all blood, was turned away from Wilder.

He was still alive, staring through the open windows at the last of the birds that the explosion had driven into the air.

Confused by this game, and its unexpected turns, Wilder stepped over him. The cine-camera lay at the bottom of the staircase, but he decided to leave it there. Rubbing his injured arm, he threw away the pistol that had jarred his hand and stepped through the french windows.

Twenty yards away, children were playing in the sculpture-garden. The doors, chained for so long to exclude them, were now wide open, and Wilder could see the geometric forms of the play-sculptures, their vivid colours standing out against the white walls. Everything had been freshly painted, and the roof was vibrant with light.

Wilder waved to the children, but none of them saw him. Their presence revived him, and he felt a surge of triumph at having climbed all the way to the roof to find them. The strange, scarred man in the blood-printed jacket lying on the steps behind him had not understood his game.

One of the children, an infant boy of two, was naked, running in and out of the sculptures. Quickly Wilder loosened his ragged trousers and let them fall to his ankles. Stumbling a little, as if he was forgetting how to use his legs, he ran forward naked to join his friends.

In the centre of the sculpture-garden, beside the empty paddling pool, a woman was lighting a large fire from pieces of furniture. Her strong hands adjusted a heavy spit assembled from the chromium tubing of a large callisthenics device. She squatted beside the fire, stacking the chair-legs as the children played together.

Wilder walked forward, shyly hoping that the woman would notice the patterns painted across his chest. As he waited for the children to ask him to play with them he saw that a second woman was standing ten feet away to his left. She was wearing an ankle-length dress and a long gingham apron, her hair drawn back off her severe face and tied in a knot behind her neck.

Wilder stopped among the statues, embarrassed that no one had noticed him. Two more women, dressed in the same formal way, had appeared by the gate. Others were stepping forward among the sculptures, surrounding Wilder in a loose circle. They seemed to belong to another century and another landscape, except for their sunglasses, whose dark shades stood out against the blood-notched concrete of the roof-terrace.

Wilder waited for them to speak to him. He was glad to be naked and show off his body with its painted patterns. At last the woman kneeling by the fire looked over her shoulder at him. Despite her change of dress he recognized her as his wife Judith. He was about to run forward to her, but her matter-of-fact gaze, her unimpressed appraisal of his heavy loins, made him stop.

By now he was aware that he knew all the women around him. Dimly he recognized Charlotte Melville, a scarf around her bruised throat, watching him without hostility. Standing next to Jane Sheridan was Royal's young wife, now a governess supervising the smallest children. He recognized the jeweller's widow in her long fur coat, her face made up like his own body with red paint. Looking over his shoulder, if only to confirm that his escape was blocked, he could see the stately figure of the children's-story writer seated in the open window of the penthouse like a queen in her pavilion. In a last moment of hope he thought that perhaps she would read him a story.

In front of him the children in the sculpture-garden were playing with bones.

The circle of women drew closer. The first flames lifted from the fire, the varnish of the antique chairs crackling swiftly. From behind their sunglasses the women were looking intently at Wilder, as if reminded that their hard work had given them a strong appetite. Together, each removed something from the deep pocket of her apron.

In their bloodied hands they carried knives with narrow blades. Shy but happy now, Wilder tottered across the roof to meet his new mothers.

19

NIGHT GAMES

Dinner was about to be served. Sitting on his balcony on the 25th floor, Robert Laing stirred the bright embers of the fire he had lit from pages of a telephone directory. The flames illuminated the handsome shoulders and thorax of the Alsatian roasting on its spit. Laing fanned the flames, hoping that Alice and Eleanor Powell, lying together in his sister's bed, would appreciate all he had done. He methodically basted the dark skin of the Alsatian, which he had stuffed with garlic and herbs.

'One rule in life,' he murmured to himself. 'If you can smell garlic, everything is all right.'

For the moment, at least, everything was highly satisfactory. The Alsatian was almost cooked, and a large meal would do the women good. Both had become querulous recently as a result of the shortage of food, and had been too tired to appreciate Laing's skill and courage in capturing the dog, let alone the exhausting task of skinning and disembowelling this huge animal. They had even complained about its nervous whimperings as Laing turned the pages of an advanced cookery book he had found in a nearby apartment. Laing had debated for some time how best to cook the dog. From the extent of its shivering and whining, the problem had communicated itself to the Alsatian, as if it was aware that it was one of the last animals in the high-rise and for that reason alone merited a major culinary effort.

The thought of the weeks of hunger to come momentarily unsettled Laing, and he fed more sheets of paper into the balcony fire. Perhaps there was game to be found on the lower levels, though Laing never ventured below the 20th floor. The stench from the swimming-pool on the 10th floor was too disturbing, and reached up every ventilation flue and elevator shaft. Laing had descended to the lower levels only once during the previous month, when he had briefly played Samaritan to Anthony Royal.

Laing had found the dying architect while chopping firewood in the 25th-floor lobby. As he pulled an antique dressing-table from the disused barricade, Royal had fallen through the gap, almost knocking Laing to the floor. A small wound had opened Royal's chest, covering his white jacket with huge bloodstains in the outline of his hands, as if he had tried to identify himself with these imprints of his own death to come. He was clearly on his last legs, eyes unfocused, the bones of his forehead cutting through the over-stretched skin. Somehow he had managed to descend all the way from the 40th floor. Rambling continually, he stumbled down the staircase, partly supported by Laing, until they reached the 10th floor. As they stepped on to the shopping mall the stench of rotting flesh hung over the deserted counters of the supermarket, and at first Laing assumed that a concealed meat-store had burst open and begun to putrefy. Appetite keening, he had been about to drop Royal and head off in search of food.

But Royal, eyes almost closed, one hand gripping Laing's shoulder, pointed towards the swimming-pool.

In the yellow light reflected off the greasy tiles, the long tank of the bone-pit stretched in front of them. The water had long since drained away, but the sloping floor was covered with the skulls, bones and dismembered limbs of dozens of corpses. Tangled together where they had been flung, they lay about like the tenants of a crowded beach visited by a sudden holocaust.

Disturbed less by the sight of these mutilated bodies – residents who had died of old age or disease and then been attacked by wild dogs, Laing assumed – than by the stench, Laing turned away. Royal, who had clung so fiercely to him during their descent of the building, no longer needed him, and dragged himself away along the line of changing cubicles. When Laing last saw him, he was moving towards the steps at the shallow end of the swimming-pool, as if hoping to find a seat for himself on this terminal slope.

*

Laing crouched over the fire, testing the hind-quarters of the Alsatian with a skewer. He shivered in the cold air flowing up the face of the high-rise, with an effort repressing his memory of the bone-pit. At times he suspected that some of the residents had reverted to cannibalism – the flesh had been stripped with a surgeon's skill from many of the corpses. The lower-level residents, under constant pressure and discrimination, had probably given in to necessity.

'Robert …! What are you doing …?' Alice's querulous voice roused Laing from his reverie. Wiping his hands on his apron, he hurried into the bedroom.

'It's all right – dinner is nearly ready.'

He spoke in the reassuring, childlike voice he had used during his hospital training with the duller of his child patients, a tone at variance with the intelligent and bored gaze of the two women in the bed.

'You're filling the place with smoke,' Eleanor told him. 'Are you sending up signals again?'

'No … it's the telephone directories. The paper must be made of plastic.'

Alice shook her head wearily. 'What about Eleanor's batteries? You promised to find her some. She's got to start reviewing again.'

'Yes, I know …' Laing looked down at the blank screen of the portable television set sitting on the floor beside Eleanor. He felt stumped for an answer – despite all his efforts, the last of the batteries had been used.

Eleanor stared at him severely. She had opened the wound on her wrist and was coyly exposing it to the cat watching with interest from the far side of the room. 'We've been discussing whether you should move to another apartment.'

'What?' Unsure whether the pantomime had become serious, Laing laughed delightedly, excited all the more when Eleanor refused to let her customary slow smile cross her mouth. The two women lay side by side, so close that they seemed to be merging into each other. At intervals throughout the day he brought them their food, but he was never sure exactly whose bodily needs and functions he was satisfying. They had moved into the same bed for warmth and security, but really, Laing suspected, so that they could synchronize their supervision over him. They knew that they were dependent on Laing. Despite the 'pantomime' their behaviour was entirely geared to meeting Laing's private needs in return for his attention to the business of their physical survival. The exchange suited Laing admirably, just as it suited him to have them in bed together – he was faced with only one set of wheedling demands, one repertory of neurotic games.

He liked to see Eleanor's old spirit emerge. Both women suffered seriously from malnutrition, and it encouraged him when they were well enough to play their parts in this loosely evolving pantomime, treating him like two governesses in a rich man's ménage, teasing a wayward and introspective child. At times Laing liked to carry the game to its logical conclusion, and imagine that it was the two women who were in charge, and that they despised him totally. This ultimate role had helped him on one occasion, when a marauding band of women led by Mrs Wilder had entered the apartment. Seeing Laing being abused, and assuming him to be Eleanor's and Alice's prisoner, they had left. On the other hand, perhaps they understood all too well what was really taking place.

Whatever the answer, Laing was free for the time being to live within this intimate family circle, the first he had known since his childhood. The situation allowed him ample freedom to explore himself, and the strong element of unpredictability kept everyone alert. Although he might wheedle at their breast he could easily become vicious. The women admired him for this. A substantial number of morphine ampoules were left, and he planned to introduce the two women to this heady elixir. Their addiction would tilt the balance of authority in his direction again, and increase their dependence on him. Ironically, it was here, in the high-rise, that he had found his first patients.

Later, after he had carved the dog and served generous but not excessive portions to the two women, Laing thought about his good fortune as he sat on the balcony with his back to the railing. Above all, now, it no longer mattered how he behaved, what wayward impulses he gave way to, or which perverse pathways he chose to follow. He was sorry that Royal had died, as he owed the architect a debt of gratitude for having helped to design the high-rise and make all this possible. It was strange that Royal had felt any guilt before his death.

Laing waved reassuringly to the two women, who sat on the mattress with the tray across their knees, eating from the same plate. Laing finished the dark, garlic-flavoured meat, and looked up at the face of the high-rise. All the floors were in darkness, and he felt happy at this. His affection for the two women was real, like his pride in keeping them alive, but this in no way interfered with his new-found freedom.

On the whole, life in the high-rise had been kind to him. To an increasing extent, everything was returning to normal. Laing had begun to think again of the medical school. He might well pay a visit to the physiology laboratory the next day, and perhaps take a supervision. First, though, he would clean up. He had noticed two women neighbours sweeping the corridor. It might even be possible to get an elevator working. Perhaps he would take over a second apartment, dismantle the barricades and begin to refurnish it. Laing thought of Eleanor's threat to banish him. He toyed with the notion, feeling an illicit thrill of pleasure at the prospect. He would have to think of something with which to win their favour again.

However, all this, like the morphine he would give them in increasing doses, was only a beginning, trivial rehearsals for the real excitements to come. Feeling these gather within him, Laing leaned against the railing.

Dusk had settled, and the embers of the fire glowed in the darkness. The silhouette of the large dog on the spit resembled the flying figure of a mutilated man, soaring with immense energy across the night sky, embers glowing with the fire of jewels in his skin.

Laing looked out at the high-rise four hundred yards away. A temporary power failure had occurred, and on the 7th floor all the lights were out. Already torch-beams were moving about in the darkness, as the residents made their first confused attempts to discover where they were. Laing watched them contentedly, ready to welcome them to their new world.